A BABY
FOR MUMMY

BY
CATHY GILLEN THACKER

MILLS & BOON

First published in Great Britain 2010
Harlequin Mills & Boon Limited,
Eton House, 18-24 Paradise Road, Richmond, Surrey TW9 1SR

© Cathy Gillen Thacker 2009

ISBN: 978 0 263 86654 4

23-1010

Harlequin Mills & Boon policy is to use papers that are natural, renewable
and recyclable products and made from wood grown in sustainable forests.
The logging and manufacturing processes conform to the legal environmental
regulations of the country of origin.

Printed and bound in Spain
by Litografia Rosés S.A., Barcelona

Cathy Gillen Thacker is married and a mother of three. She and her husband spent eighteen years in Texas, and now reside in North Carolina. Her mysteries, romantic comedies and heartwarming family stories have made numerous appearances on bestseller lists, but her best reward, she says, is knowing one of her books made someone's day a little brighter. A popular author for many years, she loves telling passionate stories with happy endings, and thinks nothing beats a good romance and a hot cup of tea! You can visit Cathy's website at www.cathygillenthacker.com for more information on her upcoming and previously published books, recipes and a list of her favourite things.

Chapter One

Dan Kingsland's mind *should* have been on business.
The catered outdoor buffet at the construction site of
One Trinity River Place was to celebrate a huge accom-
plishment, not just for his own architectural firm, but
four of his closest friends. Grady McCabe was the enter-
prising developer who'd put it all together. Travis Carson
was the contractor building the three-block office-
shopping-and-residential complex in downtown Fort
Worth. Jack Gaines owned the electronic and wiring
company that would install all the networks, phones and
satellite systems. Nate Hutchinson helmed the financial-
services company leasing seventy-five percent of the
office space.

Instead…all Dan could think about was the incredible
lunch being served, picnic-style, to the 150 high-profile
guests milling around outside the sleek stone-and-glass
skyscrapers culled from Dan's imagination. The food com-
memorating the end of Phase 1 was literally the best he had
ever tasted. And it was all being prepared by one woman,
using three portable outdoor stoves and what looked to be
an equally portable Sub-Zero fridge.

Dan savored another bite of perfectly seasoned potato salad. Maybe if they could eat like this at home…

Grady McCabe gave Dan a wry look. "We all know what you're thinking. Emily Stayton is *not* the answer to your problems."

Dan turned his gaze back to the dark-haired beauty in jeans, boots and traditional white chef's coat. The young culinary artist certainly *looked* like the solution to his dilemma. He'd lived in Texas all his life and had never had barbecue this good. The fact that Emily Stayton was literally glowing with happiness while she worked made it all the more amazing.

Dan shrugged. "The woman can cook." More important, she handled the multiple demands on her time and attention with aplomb, bringing good cheer and relative calm to the hungry crowd at the portable buffet tables.

"Of course she can cook—she's a chef," Travis said, lifting a brisket sandwich to his lips. The father of two preschoolers, he was always stating the obvious.

"She worked in the best restaurants in the area before deciding she wanted more flexibility in her schedule, and then she struck out on her own as a personal chef," Jack Gaines added with the factual precision of a guy who had founded an electronic-systems company and was single-handedly bringing up his seven-year-old daughter with seemingly none of the problems Dan was having with his own irascible brood.

"Great," Dan said, already imagining what it would be like to have this woman in his kitchen, whipping up one incredible meal after another. "That ought to make it all the easier to convince her to come and work for me." At this point, money was no object. He just wanted a solution to the problem that seemed to be growing larger every day. And if he had to think outside the box to get it, well… wasn't that what he always did? Solve problems in whatever creative way necessary?

"Not so great." Nate Hutchinson held up a cautioning hand. The only one of them with no pressing familial obligations, he made it his business to know all the beautiful, unattached women on the local social scene. And their caterer fit the bill, if the lack of wedding ring on her left hand was any indication. "Emily's leaving Fort Worth."

Frowning, Dan glanced back at the white catering van with the bright blue Chef for Hire logo on the side. "When?"

"By the end of the month. She's closing her business here this week," Grady McCabe replied. "She wants to move back to the Texas hill country, where she grew up. This is her last gig in the Metroplex."

Dan wasn't deterred by the stumbling block. He merely resolved to move around it. "Fortunately," he said, scraping up the last of the ranch-style beans, "she hasn't relocated *yet.*"

Having learned early in life that timing was everything, Dan finished his meal and waited patiently until the crowd dispersed and cleanup was under way. He walked over to the banquet tables where Ms. Stayton was busy packing up. She was not only beautiful, but her eyes were a gorgeous blue. Not that this had anything to do with his interest in her. He wanted a chef, not a wife. He was definitely not looking to get married—or even involved—again.

"I hear you're leaving Fort Worth," Dan said casually.

The knowing glance she gave him said she'd noticed him studying her—and completely misinterpreted why. She stacked empty serving dishes into a large plastic container, then went to the next banquet table to collect some more. "Yep, I'm headed to Fredericksburg."

Admiring the delicate shape of her very capable hands, Dan edged closer. "What's there?"

A mixture of anticipation and delight sparkled in her smile. "An orchard I'm in the process of buying."

As she bent over the table to reach an item at the other end, the hem of her white chef's tunic edged up, revealing the taut underside of her buttock and shapely upper thigh.

Dan tore his gaze from the delectable sight and forced himself to concentrate on the important matter at hand—her skill as a chef. "So you haven't closed on the property yet."

With a determined expression, Emily secured the top of the plastic box with a snap. She straightened and hefted the heavy container. "I will, as soon as I get paid for this gig and secure financing on the property next week. Then I'll be out of here."

Dan took the box from her and carried it to the back of the catering van. He set it where she indicated and turned back to her, noting she was about six inches shorter than his own six-two. "What about Chef for Hire?"

Emily shrugged one slender shoulder and pivoted back toward the banquet tables. To the left of them, two guys from the company that had supplied the outdoor cooking appliances loaded the equipment onto their truck. "It was fun while it lasted," she said.

Dan followed lazily, not for the first time noticing how nicely she filled out the starched white tunic. As he neared her, he inhaled the orange-blossom scent clinging to her hair and skin. The November sunshine glimmered in her mahogany hair, highlighting the hint of amber in the silky strands.

"You're going to quit, just like that, to do something else?"

"Run an orchard," she said as she gathered and folded the linens covering the tables. "And yes, I am, Mr....?"

Embarrassed he'd forgotten to introduce himself, he extended his hand. "Dan Kingsland."

She accepted his grip with the same ease she did everything else. "Nice to meet you, Dan. I'm Emily Stayton."

Surprised by how soft her hand felt, given the kind of work she did, Dan released his hold on her reluctantly. He stepped back before he could think of her as anything but a potential employee. "Lunch was great, by the way."

Her soft lips curved in an appreciative smile. "That was the plan, but…thanks."

Dan carried a stack of linens back to the van for her. "Since you haven't left yet, how does one go about hiring you?"

Her elegant brow furrowed. "For a party?"

More like…every evening. But figuring they would get to that, Dan looked her in the eye and cut straight to the chase. "I can't remember the last time my family sat down to a good dinner. Not that it was ever that great, given the lack of culinary skill in the family, even before their mom and I divorced a couple of years ago. But now, with the older two in high school and my youngest in elementary, it seems like the dinner hour has become downright impossible." He sighed heavily. "The kids are always fighting about what we're going to eat. Whereas their great-uncle Walt, who lives with us, just wants hot, home-cooked food and plenty of it."

She gave him a compassionate look. "Sounds stressful. But I'm not sure how—"

He held up a hand, urging her to let him continue. "You see, I watched you today, juggling everything that had to be juggled to feed such a large group under less than ideal circumstances. And I thought, if she could do that for us— help us figure out how to get back on the right track at meal times—maybe we'd have a chance to be a happy family again." Dan paused. He hadn't meant to reveal so much, hadn't expected anywhere near the sympathy and concern he saw in her pretty eyes.

Not sure what it was about this woman that had him putting it all on the line like this, he forced himself to go on. "So what do you say? Will you help us out?"

EMILY'D THOUGHT DAN KINGSLAND was attractive when she met him earlier, but that kick of awareness was nothing compared to the sizzle she felt when she arrived on his doorstep at six that very evening for the agreed-upon "consultation."

The single dad of three answered before she could even ring the bell.

He was dressed in boots, faded jeans and a pine-colored pullover sweater that brought out the green of his eyes. His sandy-blond hair was cut in a rumpled, laid-back style that required little maintenance. His five-o'clock shadow only added to his ruggedly handsome appeal.

He looked a bit harried, but as their eyes met and he said, "I'm really glad you came," he gave her an easy, welcoming grin.

Emily wished she felt the same ease. She sensed that if you gave this man an inch, he'd take a mile, anything to get what he wanted. Which was, apparently, a path to family peace.

Attempting a laid-back cool she didn't feel, Emily thrust her hands in the pockets of her tailored wool slacks. These days, she avoided situations that felt too...intimate from the get-go. Plus, she was a chef—not a consultant—and it was clear from the sounds of rambunctious activity in the fore-ground that his family was in the midst of end-of-workweek chaos. But in this case, money talked. She needed the extra cash the gig offered to facilitate her move back to Freder-icksburg. So she'd taken it, even though she wasn't sure what Dan expected her to be able to do here tonight.

Oblivious to the conflicted nature of her thoughts, Dan led her through the foyer to the rear of the two-story brick home. A messy, hopelessly outdated kitchen was on one side, an equally cluttered breakfast room took up the middle and on the other side of the thousand-square-foot space was a gathering room, complete with an L-shaped sofa and large stone fireplace, with bookshelves on either side. There was stuff everywhere. Briefcase. Schoolbags. Jackets and shoes and caps.

In the midst of it were his three offspring. All had his long, rangy build, sandy-blond hair and green eyes. There the similarity ended, she realized after Dan's brief intro-duction. Ava, seventeen, had her nose in a book and was busy highlighting passages with a yellow marker. Fifteen-year-old Tommy was standing in front of the fridge with the door open wide, studying the contents. Eight-year-old Kayla was dividing her time between an easel and paint-brush, and a mess of rainbow-colored modeling clay. She seemed to be working on both art projects simultaneously. Everyone seemed to be in everyone else's way and not par-ticularly inclined to do anything about it.

The little girl got up and rushed over to Emily, skidding to a stop just short of her. Washable paint dotting her arms and face, she demanded, "Are you here to cook for us?"

"Emily is here to consult with us and help us solve our problem," Dan explained. "She's going to give us some ideas on what we can eat for dinner that will make everyone happy."

"Good luck with that," Tommy grumbled. He grabbed a bottle of some sports drink from the fridge, guzzled half and started toward the door. "I'm going for a run."

Dan held up a hand. "You just got home from wrestling practice."

Tommy shrugged and plucked his sweat-dampened T-shirt away from his body. "I didn't get enough of a workout."

Emily gauged the flushed state of his skin and thought maybe he had.

"Not now," Dan repeated with paternal firmness.

Ava stood. "I don't have time for this, either. I've got to study." She picked up her heavy AP Biology textbook and highlighter.

On a Friday night? Emily wondered. Shouldn't the girl be going out with friends or just relaxing after a long week? As Emily had planned to do herself before getting waylaid by Ava's father?

Not to be outdone by her older siblings, Kayla tugged on Emily's blouse. "I've got to paint. Want to watch me?" She grabbed a brush so quickly she knocked over a jar of paint, splattering the table and floor.

Irritated, Tommy said, "Dad, make her get that stuff out of here!"

Kayla clamped her hands on her hips and tossed her long, disheveled blond hair. "I'm supposed to do my artwork in the kitchen, so I don't make a mess on the carpet!"

Ava looked up from her book long enough to put in her two cents. "Yeah, well, your stuff is in our way, as always!"

"Kids, that's enough," Dan reprimanded them just as a stiff-legged older man with a white buzz cut walked in. Dan introduced him to Emily as Uncle Walt.

Walt looked at Dan, perplexed. "I thought you were cooking tonight, Dan."

Dan shrugged. "Change of plans."

Emily looked at Dan. Had she been lured here under false pretenses?

He flattened a hand over his heart. "I wasn't going to try and rope you into it." Dan grabbed a roll of paper towels and knelt to mop up the spilled paint.

"Why not?" Uncle Walt argued, lending a hand, too. "If she can cook and she's here and it's dinnertime... Anything she makes would have to beat your cooking."

Dan took the ribbing with the affection it was given. "Thanks," he said wryly. Standing, he tossed the towel into the trash and went to wash his hands.

"It doesn't matter who cooks—meals around here suck," Tommy grumbled.

Which made Emily wonder if the kids liked the food anywhere. "What about with your mom?" she asked, curious as to whether Dan's ex had it any better when she had the kids. "What do you do for meals when you're with her?"

The room suddenly grew very silent. No one volunteered anything. Feeling like she'd plunged headlong into quicksand, Emily forged on, searching for information. "I gather meals are a problem there, too, then."

Another heartbeat passed. Then another.

Walt cleared his throat. "Didn't Dan tell you? My great-niece hasn't lived in the United States since she and Dan split up."

Chapter Two

Emily only wished Dan had thoroughly filled her in before she'd accepted this gig. If he had, she would have known this was the kind of situation that tugged on her heartstrings. And hence, one she should avoid. Now, more than ever…

"Mom's in Africa," Tommy blurted out.

"Keep up, will you?" Ava scolded, shoving her glasses up on the bridge of her nose. "That was last week. She's in China this week."

"Whatever." Tommy shrugged, edging toward the back door again. "The point is, she's not here. She's never here."

Kayla picked at the rainbow-colored volcano she had built with her modeling clay. "Yeah, we wish she would come back to see us 'cause we miss having a mommy."

Walt grimaced. "My niece is a physician for the International Children's Medical Service, or ICMS."

Which meant, Emily concluded, that Dan had full custody of their brood, with all the attendant joys and problems. As well as his ex-wife's great-uncle. This was an interesting situation.

Dan paused, his expression filled with remorse. "I'm sorry if I wasn't clear about that."

Emily slowly exhaled, belatedly wishing she hadn't asked a question that had upset the whole clan. On the other hand…what did the former Mrs. Kingsland's ongoing neglect of her kids have to do with her? Nothing, she reassured herself firmly, since she didn't expect to be here very long at all. This was Dan's dilemma—not hers!

Kayla tugged on Dan's sweater. "Dad, I need dinner now!"

Appearing frustrated he hadn't made any strides toward solving his problem, Dan silenced the complaining with a motion of his palm. "Fine. We'll order pizza."

"Not again!" the two older kids said in unison.

Dan sent Emily a look as if to say, *See what I'm dealing with here?*

Kayla stomped her foot. "But I'm really, really hungry!" she wailed as tears pooled in her eyes.

"It'll take at least an hour to get here at this time on a Friday night," Ava predicted with a beleaguered sigh.

Once a problem solver, always a problem solver, Emily thought. "How about I just whip something up?" She figured she and Dan could talk and consult while she cooked. Then she'd be able to take her paycheck and exit, before she got hopelessly enmeshed in the ongoing family drama.

"Uh…that could be a problem," Dan said.

Walt nodded. "We haven't had a chance to go to the grocery store yet."

"We only go on the weekends," Kayla said.

Emily knew people generally had more in the pantry than they thought. "Just let me have a look." She opened the fridge and realized she had her work cut out for her. They were right—pickings were meager. "I can handle it," she said confidently.

"How long is it going to take?" Kayla asked, pouting.

Emily was already assembling ingredients on the counter. "Twenty minutes."

"That's faster than we could get a pizza," Dan enthused with a grateful glance her way.

Happy a meltdown had been avoided, at least for the moment, Emily took charge. "In the meantime I need everyone to sit down with a pen and paper, and make a list of your favorite foods, along with everything you dislike, as well."

Kayla began stuffing her modeling clay back into the airtight storage containers. "Daddy, can you write mine down?"

"Will do," Dan promised.

Walt scrounged in the drawer next to the phone for pens. The older two kids sat down at the kitchen table. Emily filled a big pot with water and set it on to boil. Meanwhile, she chopped up half a pound of bacon into bite-size pieces and put all in a skillet to brown.

"What are we having?" Tommy looked suspicious.

Emily knew that to tell would only invite criticism and argument. "It's a surprise," she said with a firm smile. "Work on your lists."

Ava frowned and looked at her dad. "Can she do that?"

Dan shrugged. "Looks like she already is. Come on, everybody. This is your one chance to have a say in what we're going to have for future dinners around here."

His logic worked. Everyone got down to business, thinking, writing, thinking some more. By the time Emily put a heaping platter of spaghetti carbonara, green beans with almonds and fruit salad on the center of the table, the pages were filled.

"Hey, that looks kind of good." Tommy surveyed the fragrant pasta, sprinkled liberally with Parmesan cheese.

Kayla smiled. "Fruit salad is my favorite."

"It smells incredible," Walt said.

Dan held out a chair. "Sit down with us, please, Emily."

She hesitated. Wasn't this how she'd gotten into trouble before? By blurring the line between hired chef and family friend? "It's not—"

"Typical, I know." Dan's smile was as kind as it was chivalrous. "But these aren't usual circumstances."

Emily still would have refused had it not been for the growling in her tummy and the fact that she knew she must no longer skip meals or eat at odd hours. For the next year and a half, she had to be as conscientious about her diet as she'd been the past six months. The future of her own family was riding on that. "All right," she said gratefully. "But as soon as we're done eating, it's right back to business."

The serving platters were passed around, and then all was silent as the kids dug in. Ten minutes later there wasn't a speck of food left on the table, and Emily had made plenty.

"Wow!" Dan sat contentedly back in his chair.

Walt agreed. "Incredible."

"I didn't think I'd like that, but it was really good," Tommy said.

Ava smiled. "I liked it, too." She bolted from her chair. "Anyone want coffee?"

Dan and Walt nodded.

They didn't know how good that sounded, Emily thought wistfully. But seeing the label of the can, Emily had to decline. Caffeine was among the things she had to avoid these days, too. "Thanks. No."

"So are you going to come and cook for us all the time?"

Kayla propped her chin on her upraised hand and searched Emily's face. "'Cause I would be really, really, really happy if you did."

FOR A SECOND, DAN NOTED, Emily looked almost tempted. Then she seemed to catch herself. A hint of sadness and regret flashed in her eyes. "Oh, honey…" she began.

Dan knew she was about to decline.

Across the room, a burst of salsa music radiated from inside her shoulder bag.

Emily rose in relief, all business once again. "I apologize, but I'm really going to have to get that. I've been waiting for a call from my Realtor all day." Phone to her ear, Emily ducked out of the kitchen gracefully and walked toward the front foyer.

"You kids are on for dishes," Dan said. "Kayla, you clear, Ava, load the dishwasher, Tommy, wipe down the table and counters and take out the trash."

For once, there was no grumbling as the kids rose from the table. Maybe, Dan surmised, it was because they were all full, and hence, content—at least as far as their tummies went. Emotionally, well, it was hard to fix the absence of a mom in their lives without getting involved again, and that was something he did not want to do. His life was too complicated and busy as it was.

From the hall, Emily's voice rose in agitation.

"They can't do that, can they? I just got the okay on my mortgage application!" She sounded distraught. "Of course I can't match that! At least tell me who did this. Tex Ostrander!"

Who was Tex? Dan wondered.

Obviously the guy had some emotional connection to Emily.

Abruptly her voice cut off. Became calm and professional. "Yes. I understand. I'll talk to you in a few days."

"Wonder what's happening there?" Tommy asked beneath his breath.

Dan wondered, too, as did everyone else in his family.

Emily strode back into the kitchen. Tears of frustration glimmered in her eyes. "Sorry about that," she said in a choked voice. "I just got some really bad news." She rubbed her hand across her forehead. "Would you mind if I took your lists home tonight, studied them...and then came back again to talk to you about my suggestions?"

"Of course it's fine." Dan moved toward her. "I'll walk you out."

He waited until they reached her car, then said, "Is there anything I can do?"

Her lower lip trembling, Emily leaned against her van and turned her glance away. "Not unless you can magically buy back the Fredericksburg orchard my family owned when I was growing up." Sighing, she pushed her hand through her mahogany hair and turned her gaze to his, clearly needing to vent. "It went up for sale a few months ago. As soon as I heard, I talked to the owners. Told them I wanted it, put some earnest money down and started saving for the full down payment."

Emily swallowed and gestured ineffectually. "I mean, I knew technically that, until I secured a mortgage and made the full down payment, the owners could still receive a higher bid, though I had the right to match it—it's written into their contract with me. But I didn't really think someone would come along and offer to pay in cash—never mind my ex-fiancé!" she finished, enraged.

Dan blinked. "Your ex-fiancé just bought the orchard out from under you?"

Emily clamped her arms in front of her, the action delineating the fullness of her breasts. "He outbid me by ten percent."

Dan studied her defensive posture. "You can't match his bid?"

"Unfortunately, no." Emily moved away from the van and began to pace, her hips moving provocatively beneath the loose-fitting black trousers. "I was stretching it as it was."

Silence fell between them.

Clearly still struggling to get her emotions under control, Emily rubbed at the bridge of her nose. "The good news is since my contract with the owner is now null and void, I'll get my earnest money back, but I'm out an orchard and a mortgage application fee."

Dan held her gaze. "Why would he do that?"

Emily threw up her hands. "I don't know. I haven't seen Tex Ostrander since we broke up, and that was ten years ago."

"He knew you were buying the place?" Dan prodded, remembering how soft and silky her hands felt, despite the fact she worked with them all day.

Emily scowled and gave Dan a measuring glance. "Apparently his parents are retiring and he's decided to buy them out and move back to the area, too. If he owns both properties—the two orchards are located side by side— he'll have the biggest peach crop in the area."

And that was saying something, Dan knew, since Fredericksburg, Texas, was famous for its stellar peach crop.

Dan closed the distance between them. "So what does this mean about your move back to the area where you grew up?"

"I don't know." Emily exhaled in frustration. "My Realtor said I'm still approved for a mortgage and the bank has agreed to transfer that approval to another property."

Dan hated to see anyone lose out on a dream—particularly a deeply held one. "Maybe you could purchase another orchard," he suggested kindly.

Her lips parted as she looked up at him. "There aren't any other orchards for sale in the area, and besides, I didn't want any of those—I wanted the one my parents owned when I grew up." She kicked at the concrete drive with the toe of her boot, and Dan tried not to notice how nice she looked in profile. "I had plans to bring it back to its former glory. To… Well, never mind. It's not going to happen now." Her voice rang with disappointment. She fell silent, a morose expression on her face.

Wishing he had a way to comfort her, Dan asked, "So what now?"

Emily sighed. "It puts my plans to leave Fort Worth on hold for now. Which really sucks. Because it's the holidays, and thinking I'd be in the hill country, I turned down all these gigs I could have had."

Dan knew that catering businesses thrived during the holiday season. "There's still one you could have," he said. He resisted the urge to take her hand in both of his. "And I promise you, it will pay better than you ever dreamed."

"YOU OFFERED HER A JOB, just like that?" Walt said later that same evening when Dan filled him in on what had transpired. "Without doing a background check and getting references?"

Dan loved his ex-wife's uncle. He'd been a lifesaver the past couple years—but sometimes his negativity rankled. "Stop thinking like a private investigator."

Walt looked up from the game of Internet chess he was playing. "I'm the first to admit that the meal she made was wonderful. But we're talking about your kids here. Your home."

Dan frowned at the thought of any delay in getting things back on track at mealtime. "She was great with the kids."

As by the book as ever, Walt countered, "At least have her fill out an application—and let me talk to some of the people she's worked for in the past."

"First of all, Grady's wife has already vouched for her character. Apparently Emily has regularly catered events for the company where Alexis works. Her terrific performance is what led Grady to hire Emily for the lunch yesterday. Second, I don't think Emily has done a job like this before."

"The point is—" Walt's brow furrowed as he took in his Internet opponent's next move "—you don't know."

Dan recalled Emily's enviable ability to bring serenity even to the chaos that had ensued upon her arrival. "I don't want to blow it. Dinner tonight was the first conflict-free meal we've had in years around here."

Walt made his move with a thoughtful scowl. "Still not enough reason to hire Ms. Stayton without due diligence."

"Walt, I appreciate your sentiments. As a private investigator, you've seen things I could never even imagine. But I trust Emily Stayton." On a gut level, Dan amended silently. "And the decision is made. I want her to be our cook. Not a housekeeper, just our personal chef, for however long we can manage to get her." Hopefully in the interim he'd be able to figure out how to get Emily to come to work for them full-time. "And I don't want you doing anything to interfere with that."

Walt turned his attention back to the computer screen. "You ask me," he grumbled, "you're making a mistake."

"I didn't ask," Dan stated flatly.

Still, he couldn't help thinking about it as the night wore on.

He couldn't explain it. He just knew, on some deep fundamental level, that Emily Stayton was The One to help solve his family's problems. And Dan never discounted his instincts when they were that strong.

EMILY HAD PROMISED TO CONTINUE the consultation at nine Saturday morning. She arrived right on time. Dan went to answer the door and found her standing on the porch, much as she had the evening before—with one difference. Instead of looking pink-cheeked and healthy, she looked a little green around the gills.

"Are you okay?" Dan asked.

Emily swallowed hard, waved a vague hand, even as she moved past him. "It'll pass."

What will pass? "Are you sick?"

"Oh. No. I...I... Bathroom?" Her words were more a command for direction than a request.

Able to see what was about to happen, Dan hastened down the hall and opened the door. "In here."

Simultaneously hitting the light and the fan, she barreled past him and slammed the door. The unmistakable sounds of retching followed.

The kids came tromping down the stairs at the commotion. "What's going on?"

"Is someone…?"

"Ohhh." Tommy, Ava and Kayla looked at one another in recognition.

"Go upstairs," Dan ordered. "I'll call you."

They bolted, as was usually the case, when illness that might involve icky cleanup was involved.

"See?" Walt said, passing with his stiff-hipped gait. "You *don't* know everything about her. For all you know, she's got a problem that will leave her unable to do mornings—"

"Actually…" The door opened and Emily stepped out, still looking pale and shaky. She leaned weakly against the door frame. "Walt could be right."

Walt looked at Dan. "I'll leave you to handle this." He went into the study and shut the door behind him.

Dan guided her into the kitchen and onto a stool at the counter. "Can I get you something?" he solicited kindly. "Water? Stomach med?"

Emily regarded him gratefully. "Maybe a glass of ginger ale or a soda cracker if you have it," she said.

Dan paused.

Their eyes met.

As he worked to fulfill her request, he began to put two and two together.

"I'm pregnant," Emily said, flashing a guilty-as-charged smile.

Hence the loose-fitting shirts she wore, the fullness of her breasts in comparison to her slender figure.

"Congratulations!" Dan handed her a ginger ale and pack of crackers.

"Thanks." She ripped open the wax paper and extracted a cracker.

"How far along are you?"

She munched and sipped. "Almost four months."

"Who's the lucky guy?"

Her blue eyes glinted with unexpected humor. "76549823-CBGT."

Dan blinked. "You hooked up with a robot?"

Emily's melodious laugh filled the kitchen. Her soft lips parted as she prepared to take another sip of her ginger ale.

"A sperm bank. All I know about my baby's daddy is that he has an IQ over 140 and is Caucasian, blond, green-eyed and tall. And of course has no major inherited health problems I'd have to worry about."

Dan had lots of questions. None of which would have been polite to ask.

"I'm thirty-five, my eggs aren't getting any younger, and I wanted a family. The luck of the draw wasn't working—I just never met anyone I wanted to settle down with."

"Except Tex Ostrander." Dan recalled the name of the guy who had caused her so much grief the night before.

Emily's lips thinned. "Don't remind me. I'm still mad at him."

She didn't appear to still have romantic feelings for her ex. Although why that should matter to him, Dan didn't know. "Did you talk to him?" he asked casually, forcing himself to move on.

"No." Looking to be bouncing back from her bout of morning sickness, Emily leaned her spine against the back of the stool. "Although, not surprisingly, he called me several times. But back to the job you offered me last night—I've been thinking about it and I can't commit to a permanent family gig. It just wouldn't work out for a lot of reasons," she stated firmly. "But I could help you out on a temporary basis—until I have a chance to get some other chef gigs lined up."

This, Dan hadn't expected. He studied the new color in her cheeks and the professional competence in her eyes. "How temporary?"

"I was thinking through Thanksgiving. That would give me time to figure out what the problems are with mealtime around here—from a cooking perspective."

Maybe there weren't any, Dan thought. Maybe all they needed was a woman in the house again. "There wasn't a problem last night," he said.

Emily disregarded her success. "That was an anomaly. They were caught off guard. They were hungry. Someone set a table of hot food in front of them."

"Hot *delicious* food," Dan corrected.

Finding his mouth dry, he poured himself a glass of ginger ale, too.

"Whatever." Emily waved off the distinction. She rested both her forearms on the breakfast bar and leaned in deliberately. "The point is, these complex family issues are not going to be resolved just because I've showed up."

Trying not to be distracted by the fragrance of orange blossoms and the silk of her hair that fell seductively over her shoulder, he lounged against the opposite counter. "I think you're selling yourself short."

She mocked him with a waggle of her brows. "And I think you're minimizing the problem," she teased. "But we digress—"

Dan frowned in confusion. "Do we?"

Her gaze was completely serious now. "You haven't

said if you would be okay with the fact that I'm pregnant," she pointed out softly.

Dan's glance moved involuntarily to the slight swell of her tummy beneath the blue-and-lavender paisley tunic before returning to her face. "Why wouldn't I be?"

"I'm unmarried."

And incredibly sexy, and likely to be even sexier in a deeply maternal way as your pregnancy progresses....

"You have impressionable children," she added.

And I've had thoughts about kissing you...

He shrugged. "You're a responsible adult."

Emily raked her teeth across her soft lower lip. "Not everyone approves of what I'm doing."

Dan enjoyed the experience of being there with her, the pair of them talking with the familiar intimacy of two people who've known each other for years, instead of mere hours. He reassured her with a look. "Not everyone approves of divorce, either. Stuff happens." Old dreams fade. New ones take their place. "As far as I'm concerned, congratulations are still in order."

"Thank you." Emily smiled. "Do you think my pregnancy will bother Walt?"

Dan sidestepped the question as best he could. "He's crotchety."

Her eyes glimmered. She knew there was more. "Meaning?" she prompted.

Candor was something he could not provide. Not yet, anyway. "You don't work for him. You work for me," Dan said, and left it at that.

Emily surveyed Dan warily. "Is there something else I should know?"

Besides the fact that Walt doesn't trust anyone until a

thorough background check proves that person is trust-worthy? Dan mused. "Not a thing."

ONCE EMILY HAD fully recovered from her bout of morning sickness, they decided to get right down to business. "There's a couple ways we could approach this problem," she told the family gathered around the kitchen table.

"We're not going to be able to solve it," Tommy interrupted, evidencing the same lack of teamwork he had the night before.

Dan gave his son a stern look.

"No offense," Tommy continued, hands raised, "but none of us like the same stuff."

Emily knew sugarcoating the problems would not solve anything. They needed to examine their differences together before a remedy could be found.

"That's true, although you all seemed to like last night's dinner," Emily said. "Anyway, according to your lists, Kayla prefers mainly breakfast foods like pancakes, French toast, eggs, cereal and so on. Ava's into coffee, chocolate and salads. Tommy wants high protein and electrolytes. Dan wants anything everyone will eat. And Walt, given his choice, is a meat-and-potatoes man."

"It doesn't sound like we have anything in common." Ava sighed.

"Sure we do," Dan interrupted sternly. "We're all Kingslands."

"Uncle Walt isn't—his last name is Smith," Ava pointed out studiously.

Eager to join in, Kayla put her crayon down and piped up with, "Emily isn't one, either!"

"That's right." Emily struggled to contain control of the

family meeting. "I'm not. My last name is Stayton. It was good of you to notice that, Kayla."

Kayla beamed.

"Back to the problem," Emily said. "I can come up with menus that will please each of you. And I could make enough to feed you for several days if you wanted to eat the same thing every night, reheated."

"Leftovers?"

"I don't really like leftovers."

"Me, neither."

"Or we could draw straws to go first and take turns by night," she suggested. "That way everyone would have at least one night a week where their favorite meal was served."

The kids appeared to be thinking about this option.

"Or I could try to put one thing that everyone likes in each menu. This might make for some odd combinations. Spaghetti and scones, for instance."

All the kids made faces.

"Or we could do something a little less mundane," Emily said, more or less making it up as she went. "We could try eating a lot of new dishes from around the world. Maybe make some of the foods that your mom might be eating in her travels. We could even ask her what her favorite dishes are from some of her favorite places and try that."

The kids looked receptive to that idea. Dan did not.

"I think we should stick to the tried-and-true at first," Dan said.

The kids' enthusiasm faded and they went silent.

"If that means meat and potatoes, sounds good to me," Walt said with a shrug.

"SORRY ABOUT THAT," Emily said a short time later as Dan walked her to her van. "I didn't know you had a problem with international cuisine."

Normally Dan did not discuss his relationship with his ex-wife. Whatever went on between him and Brenda was between him and Brenda. But since Emily was going to be working so closely with his family, he figured she had a right to know. "I don't encourage the kids to try and keep up with their globe-trotting mother."

Emily looked shocked. "Why not? Surely she has e-mail and phone service."

"She does. She's just not good about using it for personal reasons. Sometimes weeks or months go by without a word from her."

"Ava knew where she was."

"Because Brenda put the two older kids on the list-serve that alerts her colleagues to her whereabouts. Getting a mass e-mail every time your mother boards a plane is not the same as having personal contact with her."

Emily appeared to mull that over. "And the lack of personal contact upsets the kids."

"It's always hard when a parent lets you down."

She nodded, for the moment really seeming to understand. Which in turn made Dan wonder what disappointments she had weathered in her life.

"I'm sorry. I didn't know," she said finally.

"Anyway," he said, "Brenda is scheduled to come home between Christmas and New Year's. Hopefully nothing will get in the way of that. Meanwhile, if we could just work on getting us on track to civilized family meals, I would appreciate it."

For the first time Emily looked uncertain. "I'm no miracle worker."

"You wouldn't have known that last night."

"Well, just so you know, I'm not here to step in and cater to their every gastronomic whim."

Dan knew that what he'd asked of her was unusual. In his estimation, that unusualness was what had made that dinner so great. "The thing is, we're not the kind of family who has servants waiting on us. I don't *want* that kind of atmosphere for my kids."

Emily tucked a strand of hair behind her ear. "Then what *do* you want?"

"Have you ever taught a cooking class?"

"Yes."

"Well, you know how, at the end of a cooking class, the chef usually sits down with the class to enjoy the food with the people she's teaching? I'm interested in creating that same convivial mood for my family during the dinner hour. Unfortunately it's something they've never really had. Even before the divorce, the meals at our house were always catch as catch can. So it's going to be like working with a group of beginners."

Sensing she was a woman who liked thinking outside the box as much as he did, Dan continued, "The point is, I'm not asking you to make a meal and serve it to us in the formal dining room. I'm asking you to create a warm, relaxed atmosphere during the meal preparation, so the kids are free to come in and out and ask questions or just hang out if they want. And if they so choose, they can learn how to cook from you. During the meal, I want you to sit down and eat with us—the way you would if you were a family friend who'd come over to help out in a pinch."

Emily made a face. "But I'd still be an *employee*."

"Only technically. As far as the kids are concerned, you are a friend of my friends Grady and Alexis McCabe, and you've agreed to help us with dinner, using your skills as a personal chef and cooking instructor." Just to be sure she knew he was serious, he named a salary that caused her eyes to widen. And still, he noted in disappointment, no sale…

"While I appreciate your offer," she said, "cooking at the same home day in and day out is not something I choose to do anymore."

"So you've worked for a single client before."

"For a few years, right after I left restaurant work. But I switched to catering small events in different venues because it was more my style."

Dan suddenly had the feeling she was holding back. Was Walt right? Was there more he should know about Emily before bringing her into his home? He decided it didn't matter. He wanted peace in his family—now—and she was the only person who could deliver it.

"Look, just give us a couple of weeks and get us through the Thanksgiving holiday," he persuaded. They both knew she had no other work lined up. And this would give her an income while she regrouped.

"Fine," Emily said reluctantly. "But the first order of business is groceries. You need a lot of staples, Dan."

So he gathered. "You want to give me a list?"

"Actually I'd like to do the shopping myself—unless you're an ace at picking out produce and know the difference between baking soda and baking powder."

"They're not the same?"

Emily winced. "No. They are not."

Dan grinned at her comical expression. "When can you start?"

"I can purchase groceries and fix dinner for you this evening."

Dan couldn't think of a better way to spend his Saturday.

"I don't work Sundays," Emily cautioned.

"What about Monday? Do you hire out for breakfast, as well?"

"How about we just do dinners to begin with?" Emily returned.

Dan knew he'd been pushing it, even getting this far. "Okay," he agreed. "What can I do to help?"

Emily rummaged through her purse for her keys. "Just be here this afternoon around four to let me in, so I can get dinner started."

That, Dan thought, sounded better than she knew.

Chapter Three

Dan was in the study, updating the plans for one of the luxury office condos of One Trinity River Place, when he heard a vehicle turn into the drive. Glancing out the window, he saw Emily emerging from her van. He walked outside, surprised by the drop in temperature. That morning it had been in the low sixties. Now he figured it had to be in the forties. And given the dark clouds on the horizon, looked to get colder still.

"See we've got a blue norther rolling in," Dan said when he met Emily at the back of the van.

She looked as if the change in weather had caught her unawares, too. Her red chef's coat and jeans were little defense against the chill wind.

Shivering, she nodded. "Guess I should have listened to the weather report."

Dan gaped at the sheer volume of food in the back of the van.

"Doesn't look like that when you shop, I gather?" Emily joked.

But maybe it should, Dan thought, noting the abundance of fresh fruits and vegetables. "When I go, it's mostly milk, cereal, bread, frozen pizzas and microwave dinners." Dan took the heavy bags from her arms. "I'll take those if you'll hold the door."

"Sure." She grabbed a bag that looked a lot lighter and moved toward the door.

Being careful not to crash into her, he led the way to the kitchen.

Once there, he was dismayed. The kids had left it in a mess, which wasn't unusual. It wasn't good, either. "Sorry," he said.

Emily sighed, looking less than pleased. She pivoted to go back to the van for more groceries. Dan stopped her with a hand to her shoulder. "Why don't you let me carry everything in? You really shouldn't be lifting anything, anyway, in your condition."

She stepped closer and stood with her hands on her hips. "That's an old wives' tale."

"Humor me?" Dan said. He let his glance rove her windswept hair, her face, before returning to her mesmerizing blue eyes.

Looking at him from beneath a fringe of dark lashes, she released a beleaguered sigh. "If you insist."

"I do. And don't touch any of those dirty dishes, either! I'll do them when I'm done carrying everything in."

That seemed harder for her to agree to, but finally she nodded her assent. He resumed his task. By the time Dan had finished, every available space in the kitchen was taken up with an overflowing bag or carton. "I've got extra freezer and refrigerator space in the garage," Dan said.

Emily was organizing the condiments, moving most to a cupboard by the sink. "We may need it." She looked around, grabbed a roll of paper towels and a bottle of spray cleaner, and mopped up some spilled milk on the counter.

Dan gathered up plates and glasses and began putting them in the dishwasher. The silence of the house was broken only by the sounds of their activity. "Where are the kids?" Emily asked finally.

Watching the play of worn denim over her slender thighs and delectably sweet butt, it was all he could do not to reach out and caress her. "Ava's with her study group, Tommy went running with a couple teammates and Walt took Kayla to a birthday party at the skating rink. But not to worry—they'll all be back in time for dinner at six."

Emily sent him a quelling glance. "What were you doing when I got here?"

Dan wiped down the tables. "Working."

Oddly, color flared in her cheeks. "Why don't you go back to it? I'm fine here on my own."

Abruptly Dan sensed Emily was as attracted to him as he was to her—and fighting it just as hard. Obviously this situation—and the intimacy it brought—was going to be a lot more difficult to navigate than he'd thought.

"Ordering me out of the kitchen?" he teased.

Emily studied him for a moment, then turned back to her work with maddening nonchalance. "I need to focus."

So did he. Because if he stayed…

"Sure," Dan said. He left, trying not to feel disappointed.

IT TOOK EVERY OUNCE OF WILLPOWER Dan had to stay out of the kitchen and out of Emily's way for the next two hours. For one thing, he was curious about where she was going to stow all the groceries she'd purchased. For another, the smells emanating from the kitchen were damned enticing. And it was his kitchen. He ought to be able to go in there whenever he wanted.

But the main thing he had to fight was his attraction to her. Being around her only increased the subtle sexual tension between them. And giving in to that attraction would not be a good thing. Especially while she was working for him.

Once things were settled in his home life, then perhaps he could see about pursuing this attraction. But for now? Emily was right to put up a wall between them and keep it there, Dan decided. It was the only logical, ethical way to proceed.

So he worked at his drafting table, and as every member of his family straggled home, he warned them not to go into the kitchen where Emily was toiling away. At six o'clock, he gathered everyone up and they headed en masse for the kitchen.

And stared, stunned, at what they saw.

EMILY WONDERED if it was all too much. The linen tablecloth and cloth napkins were nothing special—she'd borrowed them from her store of them at home. The mix of daisies and mums in the vase had come from the farmers' market.

As for the meal itself, she'd decided to go with buttermilk-brined fried chicken, mashed potatoes, corn on the cob and peach cobbler. Comfort foods in the extreme.

She figured, since the kids had welcomed the spaghetti carbonara she'd been able to throw together the night before, they were bound to like this.

She was wrong.

Maybe not wrong, exactly, she decided as the meal wore on with none of the enthusiastic eating of the trial run. But definitely misguided.

Dan, of course, consumed his meal with gusto. So did Walt. Emily was hungry, so she ate, too.

Kayla merely picked at her food, and Emily was pretty sure that Ava didn't actually taste anything. Tommy stripped the breading from the chicken, ate the meat, drank his water, and that was it.

Dan began to get irritated.

He regarded his children with the stern exasperation Emily was beginning to know so well. "What's the problem?" he asked, his tone as impatient as his manner.

Kayla shrugged. "I think I ate too much hot dogs and birthday cake at the skating rink," she said.

That excuse Dan appeared to buy.

He looked at Ava. "I had two mocha lattes while I was studying. So I'm just not hungry!"

Caffeine did cut the appetite, Emily knew.

Tommy shrugged. "I haven't completely cooled down from running. If I eat too much now, I'm likely to do what, um, Emily did this morning."

All eyes turned back to Emily. "Are you sick?" Kayla asked.

Walt, too, lifted a brow, waiting.

Dan hadn't told them, Emily realized. He seemed to not want to reveal it, either. Too bad. If the proverbial mud were to hit the fan, Emily wanted to know it now, before she invested any more in this temporary job.

"I'm pregnant—that was morning sickness," she blurted out.

HIS UNCLE GAVE DAN A LOOK that spoke volumes. Walt could clearly tell from Dan's bland reaction that he was the only one in the room who wasn't surprised by Emily's announcement.

Kayla spoke first. "Pregnant means having a baby, right?"

Dan nodded. "Right. Emily is going to have a baby approximately five months from now. And sometimes, when women are pregnant, they have tummy trouble. She had tummy trouble this morning, but that's okay—it's all part of expecting a baby." *And,* Dan's glance to his children conveyed firmly, *I have no problem with it.*

Nor did they.

In fact, the news didn't seem to faze them, either way.

"Can I be excused?" Ava said. "I really want to study some more."

"I don't feel so good." Kayla held her tummy. "Maybe I should go lie down on my bed."

"The team's going to a movie tonight," Tommy said. "I need to get ready."

Looking relieved her announcement had caused so little upset, Emily stood. "I'll clean up."

"Actually," Dan said, "I'll do it."

Emily's expression turned obstinate again. "It's my job."

He leaned forward and persisted, just as stubbornly. "Not tonight it's not. You look tired. Why don't you go on home? We'll see you Monday evening."

Emily squared her shoulders. "Are you sure?"

Dan nodded. "But you're going to need a jacket. It's really cold out there now." The wind was whipping through the trees, rustling the branches.

"I'll be fine." She moved past him in a drift of orange-blossom fragrance. "The van has a good heater."

It didn't matter, Dan thought. "You're pregnant," he reminded her protectively. He paused at the hall closet and pulled out his wind-resistant, fleece-lined hoodie. It would keep her and her baby cozy-warm. "Take this."

For once, she didn't argue. "Thank you. I'll bring it back on Monday."

He held the sleeves while she slipped it on and zipped up.

Trying not to think how feminine she looked in his jacket, despite it being way too big for her, Dan walked her to the front door.

Emily seemed flustered by the attention. "You don't have to keep doing this," she said. "I'm an employee. Not a friend. Or a—"

"Date?" Dan finished her sentence before he could stop himself.

Emily flushed as they stepped outside. In the soft glow of the porch light, she looked even prettier. "That wasn't what I meant."

On the contrary, Dan disagreed silently. It was exactly what she meant, because that was exactly how it felt—like a date. In his attempt to put her at ease, he was handling this all wrong. He swallowed, felt his throat close. "You'd rather I just stay here?"

Emily dipped her head self-consciously. "Yes."

So, with effort, Dan shoved his hands in his pockets, turned and moved to the door.

Emily got halfway down the sidewalk before she realized, "My keys! I forgot my purse." She hurried back to the door.

"I'll get it," Dan offered.

He stepped inside, Emily right behind him. Walt came out of the kitchen, a cup of coffee in one hand, Emily's leather carryall in the other. Dan recognized the look on the semiretired private investigator's face and swore inwardly.

"This what you're missing?" Walt asked Emily politely.

"Yes. Thank you. Good night, everyone! See you Monday!" Emily rushed out the door like the hounds of hell were on her heels.

In the driveway, an engine started.

Dan waited until the van drove away, then turned furiously back to Walt. "Tell me you didn't go through that," he muttered.

The older man shrugged. "Well, I had to figure out who it belonged to before I could return it to its rightful owner!"

Bull. "And?"

"She's licensed to drive in Texas. Carries two credit cards and a bottle of prenatal vitamins. Nothing incriminating in there."

The tension between Dan's shoulder blades eased. "Satisfied now?"

Walt ran a hand over his snowy-white buzz cut. "Not without references we can run down."

Dan scowled and immediately took the opposite tact. "Not going to happen," he said.

Walt looked annoyed. "Did you even ask?" he demanded in a low, disgruntled voice.

"No. And I told you, I'm not going to," Dan said, his temper rising. "I trust my gut on this."

Walt paused and shot Dan a telling look. "Make sure it's your gut and not another part of your anatomy you're following."

Dan thought about that as the evening wore on. Why hadn't he asked for references? He never hired anyone for his architectural firm without a thorough vetting. Walt's P.I. business was the one that did the work. But in this case, he hadn't even thought about it and then when prompted, had resisted the idea. Why? Why did he want to just go on emotion where this woman was concerned? He hadn't done that since Brenda. And they all knew how his refusal to deal with reality had turned out.

Back then, he'd fallen in love with a fantasy of who Brenda was, rather than who she truly was. And three kids and a divorce later, he was still paying the price. Did he really want to go back down that road?

Walt was right.

He had to delve a little deeper, even if it felt uncomfortable. Even though Emily had only agreed to be there through Thanksgiving, he still needed to be sure she was who and what she seemed.

"YOU REALLY DIDN'T NEED to do this," Emily said when she met Dan at the Starbucks just down the street from her loft on Sunday evening. He looked incredibly handsome in a charcoal-gray suede jacket and slacks, his face ruddy with cold. "We could have settled up tomorrow night after I cook dinner. Besides, it's my fault for leaving the house last night before giving you the receipt for the groceries."

Dan gestured amiably as the door to the coffee shop opened and another burst of wintry air swept in. His expression unexpectedly serious, he sat down opposite her, opened a leather portfolio and removed a checkbook. "It's not the kind of thing I want left undone."

Emily sensed there was more than that. She had gotten the impression he wanted to talk to her without his family present. She handed over the receipts from the three stores where she had made her purchases, along with the invoice from Chef for Hire, then watched as he wrote out a check. He sat back, his tall form dwarfing the café-style chair, while she slid the check into her purse.

He continued in a brisk, all-business tone. "I don't know

how you normally work, since we got together on the spur of the moment. At my firm, I have employees sign an employment contract. I assume you do the same for your catering gigs."

"Usually, yes, I do," Emily said. But this time she hadn't felt the need to put anything in writing that would have specified her pay and hours. Belatedly, she realized she should ask herself why.

Dan put the checkbook back in the portfolio and pulled out several forms. "I also generally require an updated résumé, completed application, background check and personal references."

That, Emily knew, could be tricky. "Is it really necessary?" she cut in as smoothly as she could. "Sounds expensive and laborious. And really, considering that I'll only be working for you a few weeks, quite unnecessary. Unless, of course, you've had second thoughts about having me in your home."

Dan was silent.

Emily knew that what he was asking was routine business procedure. Yet for some reason she felt insulted on a personal level. After all, he had spent enough time with her to be able to tell she was an honorable person.

He seemed to realize he had offended her. He flashed her a crooked smile meant to conciliate. "You'd almost think you had something to hide," he teased.

Actually, she did. "Ask me whatever you want," Emily said, hoping to give him enough information that a detailed check into her work history would not be necessary.

His eyes still holding hers, Dan leaned back in his chair. "What's your background?"

"I grew up in Fredericksburg, Texas. Only child. My

parents ran a peach orchard. It was sold a few years after my dad died." *For many reasons,* Emily added silently to herself, *that still upset me.* "College was out of the question at that point, so I started working in restaurants, liked it and went to culinary school, graduated and worked at three different top-tier restaurants in the Dallas-Fort Worth area until I was thirty. I got tired of the grind and long hours and branched out on my own, freelancing as a personal chef. I've done that for the last four years. And while being a solo operator has been very lucrative, it's also very demanding."

She took a deep breath before continuing. "Now that I'm starting a family, I want a less hectic life, which is why I was trying to buy the orchard. I want to be able to stay home and take care of my child as much as possible, at least for the first four or five years. I thought I had found a way to do that." She sighed. "Obviously, I haven't—since my purchase of the orchard fell through—but I'll come up with a new plan before December first."

"What happens then?" Their glances locked and they shared another moment of tingling awareness.

Emily told herself her unprecedented reaction to Dan was really just another surge of pregnancy hormones. She forced herself to get a grip. "I have to vacate my loft. It's already been rented to someone else."

"So one way or another…"

"I'll be going *some*where," Emily finished, aware her voice sounded a little rusty, and her emotions felt all out of whack, too.

Fortunately Dan had no more questions. Standing up, Emily handed him the jacket she had borrowed from him the evening before, slipped on her coat and gathered her things to leave.

Dan stood, too. "You're going to walk back to your building?"

Emily told herself not to read anything into the concern in his eyes. "It's just down the block." She slipped out the door, Starbucks cup in one hand, keys in the other.

Dan fell into step beside her. "I'd still feel better if I walked you as far as your lobby."

Ignoring the reassurance his strong male presence provided, she shrugged and turned her eyes to the awning that marked her destination. This could not lead anywhere, not if she was working for him. "Suit yourself."

They arrived at the front door of her building. Emily waved at the security man behind the desk in the lobby, visible through the double glass doors. He waved back.

"So how do you want to manage the paperwork?" Dan drawled.

Emily rocked back on her heels. "By fax. I can send you my standard agreement tonight."

Dan rocked back on his heels, too. He braced his hands on his hips, pushing the edges of his jacket back. "So you're still on for tomorrow evening?" he presumed.

Emily tore her gaze from his rock-solid chest and abs. "Absolutely. Unless we hit a snag in the paperwork, which I'm not anticipating." It was only the thorough vetting of her résumé that would reveal something Emily would rather forget. But she had an idea how to keep that from becoming a problem she would really rather not deal with. Because what happened with the Washburns was not going to happen with Dan's family. She was wiser now. Better able to keep that protective force field around her heart…

"I'll read and sign the contract right away," he promised.

Glad they had come to an agreement that was mutually

beneficial, and as thoroughly professional as it should have been from the beginning, Emily nodded. "Thank you."

Another peaceful moment passed between them. Emily smiled and began to relax. Maybe this would work out, after all, she thought. And, of course, that was the moment the next unwelcome complication arose.

Chapter Four

Emily went pale as a dark-haired man, roughly their age, climbed out of a pickup truck parked in front of her building and strode toward them. In a white western shirt, jeans and black leather jacket, he appeared to be both sophisticated and affable.

He touched the brim of his black Resistol hat and stopped just short of them. "Emily," he said, smiling and looking her up and down. "It's been a while."

Emily stood her ground and made no move to greet the interloper with anything even faintly akin to the same familiarity and warmth. Instinctively Dan slid a protective arm behind her.

"Ten years," Emily acknowledged, her voice taut. Turning slightly, her elbow brushing Dan's ribs, she looked up at Dan and said, "Dan, I'd like you to meet Tex Ostrander."

Her ex-fiancé. The man who'd bought the orchard out from under her and thrown her life into chaos.

"Tex, this is my, um, friend—" she stumbled slightly over the misnomer "—Dan Kingsland."

Aware Emily was using him to keep her ex at bay, Dan played along and extended a palm. "Nice to meet you."

"Same here," Tex said.

As the two men shook hands, Dan noted Tex had a firm, no-nonsense grip.

"What are you doing here?" Emily demanded.

"We need to talk about my purchase of the orchard," Tex said. "And since you wouldn't return my calls…"

Emily frowned in warning. "I can't imagine we have anything to say to each other."

Tex clearly differed. "Do you really want to discuss business out on the sidewalk?" Tex asked.

A group of teens walked by, talking and laughing.

Emily's frown deepened. She looked at Dan, a question in her eyes. Getting the hint—she wanted and needed a neutral third party to possibly run interference for her—Dan wordlessly agreed to help her out. He stipulated mildly, "As long as it doesn't take too long. Emily and I have plans for this evening." *Just not together.*

Incorrectly assuming Dan was Emily's date and he was interrupting something, Tex shrugged. "I'm fine with that. I just want a chance to explain and make my pitch."

The three of them walked inside and took the elevator to Emily's loft. The high-ceilinged, brick-walled abode had a bank of windows overlooking the Trinity River. The thousand-square-foot apartment was divided into four areas—work space, living room, kitchen and bedroom. The only space walled off was the bathroom at one end.

She led them to the stylish sofa and a pair of chairs at one end of the room. She sat down on the sofa. Dan sat next to her.

Tex took one of the sling-back chairs opposite them. "I'm here to offer you a job," Tex said.

Emily looked as if she could hardly believe Tex's temerity. Nor could Dan, under the circumstances.

Emily stared at Tex. "You really think I'd accept a job from you after what you just pulled?"

Tex nodded. His expression earnest, he continued in a flat, practical tone, "We both know the only reason you wanted the orchard was to bring it back to its former glory. You don't have the money or the agricultural background to make the sort of improvements required. But I do. And since my parents are retiring to Arizona and have recently sold their orchard to me, and the properties are side-by-side, it makes good business sense to merge the two and have one operation with twice the capacity, rather than two competing businesses."

As much as Dan was loath to admit it, Tex's pitch made sense, from a business perspective, anyway. Personally, it was another matter indeed.

Emily frowned, looking tempted despite her earlier refusal. "What are you offering me exactly?"

"A full partnership if you'll agree to defer most of your salary in exchange for equity, just as I am, until we get the new business up and running. Bottom line—I'm only going to be around part of the time. I need someone I trust to live on the property and run the orchards when I'm not there, and start an on-property restaurant-slash-retail-business that will feature fresh fruit, preserves, pastries, salsas and whatever else you can dream up to produce with our crops."

"Why me, Tex? Why not someone else?"

"Because you're the only one who knows how much blood, sweat and tears went into starting these orchards. Together, you and I can make them better than either of our folks ever dreamed. So what do you say, Emily?" Tex leaned forward urgently, hat in hand. "Can I count on you? Are you in?"

"THANKS FOR STAYING," Emily told Dan several minutes later, after Tex had left.

Dan looked around her loft. The sleek, minimalist space didn't seem to jibe with her any more than Tex Ostrander did. She seemed much more at home in his traditionally cozy kitchen.

"No problem," Dan said. He had wanted to make certain she was all right. He watched as she walked to the stain-less-steel island that served as both work surface and dinner table. She plucked an orange from the fruit bowl and began to peel it with single-minded concentration.

"Are you going to accept Tex's offer?" Dan asked.

"I don't know." She offered Dan half the orange. "On the one hand, I'm really ticked off about the way he sub-verted my dream."

"But not surprised," Dan guessed as he popped a section of orange in his mouth.

Emily made a face. "He's always been ambitious to a fault. It was never going to be enough for him to help run his parents' orchard until they decided to retire."

Curious, Dan asked, "Is that why you two never married?"

Emily downed one orange section, then another. "We got together when my mom died and I needed someone to be there for me. He stepped in and provided the sta-bility and direction I needed at a time when just trying to decide whether or not to continue subscribing to the daily newspaper was a quandary." She met his gaze. "When my grief ebbed and I no longer needed someone to solve all of life's problems for me, I realized some-thing else that had eluded me. He was always going to put his own needs first and think that his dreams were more important than mine. And that hurt." Her eyes narrowed. "And he's obviously still behaving in that manner—for example, thinking he's doing me a favor by buying the orchard out from under me, because he can run it better than I can."

"I sense a 'but' in there somewhere."

She looked in the fridge. It was crammed with all manner of fresh fruit and vegetables. She moved the milk and cheese and withdrew a jar of dill pickles. Dan shook his head at her offer.

She withdrew a pickle for herself and recapped the jar. "Bottom line—I still want a hand in restoring the property where I grew up." She took a bite of the pickle, catching the dripping juice with one hand cupped beneath the other. Appearing as if the sour taste were heaven—and who knew, maybe it was to a pregnant woman—she continued, "And the thought of having the money to start a restaurant and a line of peach, strawberry, blackberry and plum products with my family's name on it is tempting."

Dan studied the glitter of excitement in her eyes. "Even if it means working closely with your ex?"

Emily turned on the spigot and washed her hands with lavender soap. Some of her pleasure faded. "I think I can handle Tex."

Dan ignored the stab of unaccustomed jealousy and pointed out, "You didn't seem that sure earlier." He watched as she dried her hands with a towel, determined to let her have her say. "When you were pretending I was someone of significance in your life."

Emily flushed, as if guilty as charged. She helped herself to a wrapped candy on the counter, then pivoted toward him. The tantalizing drift of orange-blossom perfume teased his senses. "First of all," she corrected archly, "I never actually said that."

She hadn't needed to. Tex had gotten the message and jumped to the necessary conclusion.

Dan waved off her offer of a candy. "It was implied, in the way you introduced me as your 'um, friend.'"

She removed the foil wrapper from the treat and popped it in her mouth. Dan watched her savor it. Her eyes locked with his, she lifted her shoulders in an aimless shrug. "You could have refused to go along with it."

"And desert a damsel in distress?" he retorted. "I don't think so."

The color in her cheeks went from pink to rose. "Whatever." She waved off Dan's concern. "It's no longer necessary now that I know why Tex did what he did."

"Sure about that?" Dan took comfort in the fact that Emily hadn't given Tex an answer, had merely said she wanted to think about it before deciding.

"What are you insinuating?" she demanded, apparently annoyed.

Aware he did not want to be shown the door as readily as Tex had just been, Dan shrugged and voiced his theory about what was really going on here. "Maybe this is all a ruse to get you back. Maybe Tex is still interested in you— romantically." Certainly Dan couldn't imagine letting Emily go without a fight if she was his woman.

"Don't be ridiculous!" Emily scoffed. "Tex and I haven't been in contact with each other for ten years!"

"Plenty of time for him to realize he made a mistake and want to make amends." And what better way than by being an integral part of Emily's dream of restoring her family's farm to its former glory?

Emily sighed resentfully. "That's *not* going to happen."

"Why not?" Whatever the answer, Dan needed to hear her say it.

She folded her arms in front of her, the action accentuating the fullness of her breasts and the slight roundness of her tummy. "Because I'm not interested in Tex."

The look on her face made him a believer. His heartbeat kicked up. "Not that it should matter to you either way," Emily added bluntly.

Yeah. Well… "It does," Dan shot back just as bluntly.

"Why?" she asked.

Aware she was close enough for him to see the turbulent emotion in her eyes and note the slight unsteadiness of her breathing, Dan retorted gruffly, "Because I don't want to see you—or your baby—hurt." And whether Emily realized it or not, this situation with Tex had the potential to do just that.

"So you're what now?" Emily tossed back. "My unofficial protector?"

Aware that put him in the class Tex had been in—and look where that had gotten the man—Dan exhaled slowly. "And then some," he murmured back.

She stared at him in confusion.

And then he did what he had been wanting to do from the first moment they'd met. He forgot all the reasons they shouldn't tear down boundaries, took Emily in his arms and pulled her against him. She tipped her head back with a soft, anticipatory "Oh!", which propelled him to continue. Caution fled as he cupped the back of her neck with one hand and slanted his mouth over hers. She moved against him provocatively as their mouths met. After that all was lost in the scent and touch and feel of her. Her lips were warm and mobile, and she tasted like chocolate, peppermint and woman. The fullness of her breasts, the slight roundness of her tummy pressing into him, increased his desire. Dan stroked his hands up and down her spine, and let himself fall even further into the kiss, aware all the while of the steady rhythm of her heart against his.

Emily hadn't intended to give in to the simmering attraction any more than she had meant to lean on Dan's solid, reassuring presence when Tex showed up. But from the moment he touched her, her spirits rose. There was just something about Dan that she could not resist. That left her wanting to know and experience more.

Like this kiss. Maybe it was because she was pregnant and had been alone for what seemed like forever, but Emily had never felt such pure, unadulterated passion, never wanted a man more than she did at this moment. He used no pressure, yet she felt overwhelmed. Persuaded. Seduced. And the fierce ardor welling up inside her was reason enough, she knew, to break off the sweet, steamy embrace.

Reminding herself that, like it or not, Dan was still her employer and, hence, she needed to exhibit at least a little common sense, Emily put her hands on his chest and pushed.

Dan lifted his head, his eyes dark with desire. Breathing hard, flushing with a heat that started deep inside and radiated outward, Emily stepped back.

She noted with chagrin there wasn't an ounce of regret in his demeanor. *Or in her heart.* Her mind, however, was a different matter.

"That," she said flatly, calling on every ounce of inner fortitude she had, "was a mistake that can't happen again. I work for you."

HER TREMBLING WORDS were a shock to his system. As much as Dan was loath to admit it, Emily was right. She was his employee. There would be time to pursue this attraction when that was no longer the case. Right now, there were larger problems to address.

He still needed to bring order to his family's mealtimes—and like it or not, she was the key to that.

Emily needed to figure out what she was going to do after December first. And with Thanksgiving coming up… Concentrating on the two weeks between now and the holiday seemed best.

"I crossed a line I shouldn't have," he admitted reluctantly.

Emily sighed and pushed her hands through her hair. "We both did."

"So what do you say?" he prodded.

"Want to just forget it? Pretend—" she paused and briefly averted her eyes "—it never happened?"

Dan nodded, knowing even as he bid her good-night and left that it wasn't that simple. That kiss had been seared into his memory, and, he suspected, hers, too.

Fortunately the house was quiet when he got home.

Kayla was already asleep, the older two kids ensconced in their rooms. Walt was in the study, printing out photos for a client.

Dan noticed the digital pictures coming out of the printer. One glance told him why Walt had waited to print until the kids weren't around. "Another cheater?"

"Unfortunately. Client's not going to be too happy. On the other hand, she'll be relieved to find her husband's infidelity was not a figment of her imagination, as he claimed." Walt indicated the machine connected to the phone. "You had a fax come in a few minutes ago."

Dan plucked the pages out of the feed. It was from Emily. She hadn't wasted any time completing the paperwork and sending him a copy of her agreement. Dan wished her timing had been better. He turned back to Walt. "I imagine you looked at this?"

Walt nodded. "With the exception of your friend Grady McCabe all her references are from the restaurant work she did four to ten years ago."

Before she became a personal chef for hire. Dan scanned the pages Emily had sent, relieved to note that nothing else looked out of the norm. "We discussed that."

Walt ran a hand over his hair. "And?"

She hedged in a way that made him want to back off, for both their sakes. Once again going with his gut, Dan shrugged off his uncle's concern. "I trust her," he said flatly. He held up a hand before Walt could interject. "But to make you feel better, I'm giving you the okay to do a routine background check."

Finally Walt was happy. "Want me to follow up with the references, too?"

Dan nodded. "But don't go overboard," he cautioned. He knew his uncle. The years as a private investigator had left Walt seeing trouble around every corner. And trouble was something Dan did not want to find. Not now, and certainly not before the Thanksgiving holiday.

To Emily's relief, Dan filled out the paperwork as quickly as she did. She reported for work on Monday afternoon at four. Determined to meet the needs of the Kingsland family without becoming emotionally involved with Dan and his kids, Emily set about preparing nutritious after-school snacks to hold the kids until their six-o'clock dinner. And immediately hit a snag.

"I can't do my homework," Kayla told Emily when she got home from school.

Although child care was not part of her job description, Emily reminded herself, creating a warm and welcoming environment for them was. She set a snack of apple slices and yogurt dip in front of Kayla.

"Why not?" Emily cut shortening and salt into flour and added just enough water to make dough.

As if she had no appetite whatsoever, Kayla glumly pushed the dish away. "Because we have to ask our parents what their Thanksgiving traditions were when they were our age, and my mommy isn't here."

"She has e-mail, doesn't she?" Emily asked as she put golf-ball-size rounds in the cast-iron tortilla press.

"Of course Mom has e-mail," Ava said, walking in the door, heavy backpack of books in one hand, a tall iced latte in the other.

"Do you know the address?" Emily asked, determined to solve the problem before it became a full-blown catastrophe that would interfere with the dinner hour.

Ava sat down at the desk in the kitchen and switched on the personal computer. A series of key clicks later, she had logged on to the Kingsland-family e-mail and started a new message for Dr. Brenda Kingsland. "There you go." Ava grabbed her backpack and coffee and exited.

"Dinner's not for another two hours," Emily called after Ava's retreating figure. "Do you want a snack?"

"Nope. Not hungry!" Ava responded without turning around.

Kayla wrapped her arms around Emily's waist. "Will you type the message for me?"

Knowing the task was beyond the eight-year-old's capability, Emily smiled. "Sure," she said.

A few minutes later, it was done.

The question had been sent, and Kayla began happily munching the apple slices Emily had prepared.

DAN WALKED IN AT SIX to find a make-your-own-taco bar had been set up on the kitchen counter. Emily was standing at the stove flipping fresh flour tortillas on a griddle while the rest of his family, drawn by the delicious scents filling the house, made their way into the kitchen. The scene was cozy and welcoming, despite the continuing lack of total cooperation from his children.

"I thought we'd fill our plates buffet-style," Emily told everyone. Her cheerful smile buoyed Dan's spirits even more than when Walt had let him know—first thing that morning—that the routine background check had turned up nothing at all. There wasn't even a parking ticket on Emily's record.

"I'm not all that hungry," Ava announced, tossing her empty latte cup in the trash.

"Maybe some salad topped with a little meat and cheese?" Emily suggested gently.

"I guess I could do that." Ava reluctantly headed up the buffet line.

Dan relaxed as some of his eldest daughter's recalcitrance faded away. The air of serenity falling over the kitchen was exactly what he had envisioned.

"Will you make mine?" Kayla asked Emily from her perch at the computer keyboard in the kitchen. Behind her, the e-mail screen glowed.

"Sure," Emily said, beckoning Kayla to her side so the little girl could show her what she wanted.

Tommy—who had showered after wrestling practice for once—added spicy beef, greens, pico de gallo and black beans to his plate, passing on the rice and tortillas.

Walt showed no such restraint—he loaded up his plate with a bit of everything, including the freshly made guacamole and sour cream. Stomach rumbling, Dan followed suit.

"Is your baby going to be a girl or a boy?" Kayla asked when Emily had fixed a plate for herself and sat down.

Although technically it was none of his business, Dan had wondered as much himself.

Emily's face lit up, the way it always did when she spoke about her baby. "I don't know yet," she said.

Ava leaned forward eagerly. "Are you going to find out?"

Emily nodded. "In a couple of weeks, when I have my ultrasound."

"What's an ultrasound?" Kayla asked.

Emily briefly explained the procedure. "I'll bring a picture so you can see. That is—" she flushed and looked at Dan "—if it's okay."

A lot of things were okay, Dan thought. Including Emily's presence there with them. "Sure," he said.

At the kitchen desk, the mail icon sounded with a little ding. Kayla got up so quickly she knocked her chair over. "Look!" she shouted in excitement. "It's a message from Mommy!"

"I WISH YOU HADN'T done that," Dan said as he walked Emily out to her van after dinner.

Emily could see that in the implacable set of his mouth and the disapproval in his eyes. She also thought Dan was wrong. "Kayla got the information she needed, as well as a promise that her mom would try to call the kids tomorrow, talk with them."

His handsome jaw took on the consistency of granite. "A promise that Brenda might not keep."

Emily shrugged. "And that she very well might."

Dan eyed her like a grizzly on a bad day. "Look, I gather you meant well…but my kids have been hurt enough by their mother's abandonment."

Emily turned up the collar on her coat to ward off the chill of the November evening. "And you think you're helping them by encouraging their low expectations of their mom."

Dan looked at the half-moon in the dark night sky. "I'm encouraging them to be realistic."

Emily leaned against the side of her van and folded her arms in front of her. She knew she risked overstepping her bounds by getting involved in this, but she had to speak her mind. "Even if it devastates them in the end? Brenda works in dangerous parts of the world. She could easily succumb to illness, earthquake, flood or heaven knows what else. You don't want their last thoughts of her to be angry, or for their last contact with her to be hurtful. You don't want your kids to have to carry that kind of burden for the rest of their lives."

Dan paused. "Are we talking about them now, or you?"

"Both, I guess."

He waited.

Emily sighed. She supposed it wouldn't hurt to explain. "My dad was a fantastic businessman and farmer. He grew the Stayton Orchard from nothing. Whereas my mom was dependent on him for literally everything. When my dad died, she fell apart and let the business go all to hell in just a couple years. She destroyed the legacy he'd built, my college funds, everything. I was furious with her when she sold the farm. I hitched a ride to Fort Worth with a friend who went to college here, got a job in a restaurant and didn't look back." Emily shoved a hand through her hair and continued miserably. "Two years later Mom died of complications from pneumonia. Although at the very end we were able to see each other and express our love for each other, I still can't forgive myself for all the time we squandered. I can't forgive myself for not taking the time to understand things better from her point of view."

Dan moved close enough to search her face. "Which is what you think my kids should do."

"Yes—for everyone's sake. It's not as if they're not suffering as it is. Ava's studying nonstop and living on coffee, probably in an attempt to emulate her mom and so feel worthy of her attention. Tommy is channeling all his excess emotion into his physical training, which in itself isn't bad. But he's overexercising and eating just enough to get by to maintain his weight for wrestling, which leads me to think maybe he's in the wrong weight class. And Kayla can't eat whenever she misses her mommy or wants extra attention from you to make up for it, which is a lot, frankly."

He rubbed his jaw contemplatively. "You picked up on all that?"

Emily exhaled in frustration. "It's easier for me. I'm not a member of the family, so I'm able to be more objective about what's making your mealtimes so generally miserable. And it's not really that they can't agree on a menu," she said more quietly after a moment. "It's that they miss having a mom here with them." To the point that Emily's own heart ached for them.

"What do you think I should do?" Dan asked eventually, bracing his shoulder against the side of the van.

"For starters?" Emily retorted wryly. "Tell them what you and I have been talking about all this time."

Dan's brows knit together in confusion.

"Don't look up," she said softly. "But there are three very inquisitive children watching us out their bedroom windows."

Chapter Five

Emily was not surprised to receive an e-mail from Dan first thing the following morning. By 9:00 a.m., he was at her door, looking incredible in a dark green suit, pale olive shirt and contrasting tie.

"Thanks for making time to see me this morning," Dan said, his deep voice sending a thrill coursing through her.

"No problem." Reminding herself this meeting was strictly business, Emily ushered him into her loft and shut the door behind them. She led him to the breakfast bar in the kitchen area, where she'd set up decaffeinated coffee service for two. She stepped behind the counter and went back to whipping up a batch of apricot scones. "I've been curious about what you said to your kids last night."

Dan watched as she cut butter into a mix of flour, sugar, baking powder and salt. "For starters, I told them it's not polite to spy on two people having a conversation, and then I talked to them one on one about what's been going on. Ava admits she's overdoing it on the caffeine, but says it's the only way she can keep up the energy she needs to study." He exhaled slowly. "Tommy acknowledges he is being careful about his weight, but says there's no spot for him in a heavier weight class, and so at least for the rest of the season he's just going to have to continue to maintain his current weight. And Kayla still thinks Brenda is going to call her."

"And you don't." Emily combined cream with beaten egg and then folded it into the mixing bowl with the other ingredients.

Dan compressed his lips. "Let's put it this way. There have been many more promises broken than kept."

Emily stirred in the fruit. "Maybe Brenda will come through this time."

"And maybe she won't. Maybe she'll do what she always does," he said bitterly, "and make a grand entrance and present them with ridiculously lavish gifts meant to make up for all the times she's not been there for them."

Emily turned the dough out onto a floured surface. "Does that work?"

Dan watched her roll the dough out into a circle and cut it into eight triangles. "Initially, no—the kids were so angry they refused to accept anything she gave them. After a couple of years had passed, their need to punish her faded and they slowly began to warm up to her again—albeit in a sort of emotionally distant way."

That sounded sad, Emily thought. She slid the baking pan into the oven and set the timer for fifteen minutes. "How old were the kids when Brenda left?"

"Ava was thirteen, Tommy eleven and Kayla barely four. As you can imagine, Kayla had the hardest time. She just couldn't understand why her mommy was going away like that—that she wouldn't see her for months on end."

Dan drained his coffee cup and Emily reached across the counter to refill it. "It would have been one thing had

Brenda been in the military and had no choice," Dan went on, then shook his head. "But Brenda signing on full-time with ICMS was strictly voluntary."

"And hence hurt everyone, especially Kayla."

Dan nodded. "So in the future, please refer Kayla to me if she needs to contact her mother."

"All right."

Dan rested his elbows on the counter. "As for Ava…I'm not sure what to do."

Emily carried the dirty dishes to the sink. "You can forbid her to use caffeine."

Dan's smile softened. "I'd rather she come to the right conclusion on her own."

"Which is where I come in," Emily guessed dryly.

His eyes followed the swift movements of her hands. "With her knack for science and your ability to cook…I was hoping you could convince Ava to collaborate on some research into the best way to fuel her body for studying. The same with Tommy, only his focus is optimum athletic performance." He sighed. "I know it's a lot to ask, but if we could come up with lists of food that would work for both of them and add those to our menus…"

"You'd have the happy dinner hour you crave?"

"Exactly." Silence fell, more comfortable this time.

"What about Kayla?" Emily asked at last.

Dan kicked back on the stool, his expression pensive. "She takes a lot of her cues from her older siblings. If they're happy, she's in a much better frame of mind, too."

Needing to rest for a moment, Emily came around the breakfast bar and took a stool two down from Dan. She sipped her decaf. "I'll give it my best shot, at least for the next couple weeks."

Dan glanced at the papers and photos spread out at the end of the breakfast bar. "What's all that?"

"Specs for the Stayton-Ostrander Orchard. Tex e-mailed them to me late last night. He asked me to spend some time looking at them before I make up my mind."

Dan frowned. "What'd you think after looking at it?"

"He makes a good case, that together we'll do a lot better than either of us would alone."

"But…?" His expression was as maddeningly inscrutable as his posture.

"I'm still angry about the way Tex went about this, purchasing the property out from under me with a bid he had to know I couldn't match."

"It does seem if had he wanted a true partner, he would have talked to you first."

Emily traced the rim of her coffee cup with her fingertips. "Exactly."

Dan studied her. "And yet you remain torn."

The compassion in his eyes made it easy to confide. "My father put everything he had into that orchard. It broke my heart when my mother had to let it go. I've felt guilty for years about what happened."

"Why?"

"Because I didn't try to intervene when I knew she was making bad business decisions."

Dan shook his head. "You were just a kid."

"I still could have helped more. Done the research, gathered information, presented it to Mom. It might have made a difference. Instead, I sat back and judged her for everything she did wrong. I should have worked by her side every chance I had to rescue the family business. Finally I have a chance to do something about it, bring it back to its former glory."

"But that means working closely with Tex."

Emily inhaled, taking in the brisk wintry scent of Dan's aftershave. "And I'm not sure I want be in business with someone who constantly thinks he knows what's best for me."

Dan inclined his head. "Signing on as Tex's partner could mean a perpetual power struggle," he agreed.

"But—" Emily bit into her lower lip "—it's also a way to honor my father and make up for my mother's mistakes and my inaction."

"So you're tempted," Dan concluded.

Emily's throat was thick with emotion. "You don't know how much."

THREE HOURS LATER, DURING a pickup game of basketball at the club, Dan was still thinking about the situation. It didn't take long for his friends to notice his distraction. Predictably, after three missed shots in a row, they called him on it.

Reluctantly Dan explained.

Grady dribbled past him. "I can see why you're bummed, thinking Emily might go into a partnership with her ex-fiancé," he said.

"But whether or not such a move is going to be a mistake for Emily is not your problem," Travis reminded him.

Then why did it feel like his problem? Dan wondered. It wasn't as if he and Emily were dating or anything. She was a temporary employee, and a remarkably independent one at that. Just because they'd once had the bad judgment to give in to the physical attraction between them, did not make him her Sir Galahad.

Jack sped past, ambidextrously dribbling the ball. "You

have to stay focused, pal. Think about the fact that you need a cook for your family."

"One," Nate added, springing up and catching the rebound with his usual skill, "who gets along with your kids."

"So if it's not going to be Emily, because she feels she has to pick up the banner on behalf of her family…" Grady winced with displeasure as his shot hit the backboard before falling in with a swoosh.

"Then find someone else," Travis concluded.

Easier said than done, Dan thought as the day progressed.

He'd employed enough people in his architectural firm to know that hiring a person with the right skills was one thing. Hiring someone with the right skills who was also capable of seamlessly blending right in was a rare thing indeed.

The simple truth of the matter was that Emily meshed with his family. And although his kids weren't wildly enthusiastic about her presence—yet—at least they hadn't gone all out to drive her away. Which meant he had to do everything in his power to convince her to stay on as long as possible.

His mind made up, Dan showered quickly and headed back to the office. Once there, he quickly settled into a meeting with his staff, discussing the proposed changes to the interior design of a just-sold penthouse condominium at One Trinity River Place. They were deep into a discussion of how the sun would affect the new design when Dan's secretary stuck her head in the door. "Sorry to interrupt, boss," Penny said, "but Dr. Kingsland is on the phone. She said she's about to board a bus into the Changbai mountains and the connection is really bad."

"Keep going," Dan instructed his staff.

He slipped out of the conference room. Penny strode

briskly beside him. "The front desk just phoned to let me know that Walt and Emily Stayton are on their way up."

Dan did a double take. What was *that* about?

Penny motioned toward the phone on his desk, and, figuring first things first, Dan strode to the receiver. "Brenda?" he said.

"I don't know who this Emily person is, but honestly, Dan, don't you think you could have consulted me before…" Crackling cut off whatever else Brenda said.

"…I'm coming home as soon as I get done with my work in the mountains…." More static. "I know I said Christmas…but it's going to be Thanksgiving. I've already told the kids…" More snapping sounds. "…an old-fashioned holiday…no restaurants this year…going to cook…"

The line went dead just as Walt and Emily walked in.

Emily looked as perplexed as Dan felt, but Walt's expression was choirboy innocent.

Another bad sign.

"What's the emergency?" Emily asked, still appearing slightly out of breath, like she'd hurried to get there.

Dan speared Walt with a look that let him know this better be good. "I'd like to know that myself," he drawled.

Emily blinked. "You didn't call this meeting?" she asked, suddenly ill at ease.

"Actually, I called it," Walt said.

And Dan had a sinking feeling he knew why.

EMILY WHIRLED TO FACE the older man beside her. In sport coat and tie, his cheeks ruddy with the cold winds currently blowing through the city, he looked like a TV-show cop about to escort a suspect to the interrogation room.

"I looked into your background," Walt told Emily. "Found out your first personal-chef job was with the Washburn family, and that you were there for over a year. I was curious why you would have left that off the résumé you gave to Dan, and so I called Stu and Sylvie Washburn to see what kind of recommendation they would give you." He quirked a brow. "Surprisingly, they refused to talk to me at all. Said they wanted to put the whole sorry episode behind them and move on, and they hoped you had done the same. Naturally I wanted to give you a chance to explain."

Her face burning with embarrassment, Emily glanced at Dan. He appeared as stunned as she was by what was transpiring.

Dan blew out an exasperated breath. "You should have talked to me first," he told Walt in a way that made Emily feel all the worse.

Walt refused to back down. He folded his burly arms in front of him and continued just as stubbornly, "I knew when you stopped letting a pretty face cloud your judgment and came to your senses, you'd realize these questions need to be answered before Emily sets foot in your home again."

The last thing Emily ever wanted to do was cause trouble within another family again. She stepped between the two men as they faced off. "It's all right. I don't mind explaining. It's just I had hoped not to revisit the situation. It's the only time in the eighteen years I've been working that I've ever been fired. And I guess it still smarts."

Dan looked at Emily. "What happened?" he asked gently.

Still feeling a little like she was caught in the middle of a good cop–bad cop game, Emily set her shoulder bag on the floor beside her. Feeling way too warm, she slipped off her coat and scarf and draped them over the back of the chair. Her spine straight, she lifted her chin and continued speaking to both men.

"I was really tired of restaurant work at that point. The stress and long hours and the bickering between all the high-strung personalities had really worn me down. The job with Stu and Sylvie seemed tailor-made for me. They were both high-powered executives. They had sophisticated palates, as did both their twin girls, who were ten. They traveled frequently, so the job was live-in. My duties were only to cook, shop and clean up after meals. They had staff for everything else.

"And at first it was ideal. I worked seven days a week, but I had plenty of time off each and every day to do whatever I wanted. But then—I guess it was about three months into the job—their nanny quit, and I temporarily took on the job of helping the twins with their homework after school. Stu and Sylvie went through the motions of trying to find someone else, but the girls liked me—and I liked them—and so eventually it was decided that I would take an increase in pay in exchange for supervising the girls when their parents weren't around, which ended up being all the time."

She looked away. "The three of us began to get close. I really loved them, and the girls came to love me. Turns out, Stu and Sylvie weren't happy about that. They sat me down and reminded me to remember my place." Emily winced, recalling that uncomfortable meeting.

"That doesn't sound particularly nice of them," Dan said.

"You'd think, since you were caring for their children, that they would want you to be loved and respected by their kids," Walt agreed.

Emily shrugged, facing the two men again. "They had a

point. I might have felt like family to the girls, but I wasn't, so I tried to step back emotionally. But that upset the girls because they didn't understand the change in my attitude— so I was perpetually on this tightrope trying to behave in a compassionate and supportive manner and yet not love them as my own, which was tough as hell because they were great kids and I was tremendously fond of them." Emotion filled her voice. "Anyway, I knew it was a bad situation for all of us, and I kept thinking I should leave, but then I also kept thinking what would happen to the girls if I did."

Dan's eyes filled with compassion. "What an awful position to be in. So what happened next?"

"It all blew up in our faces because Stu and Sylvie over-heard the twins talking about how they wished I was their real mommy, not Sylvie. I was fired that same afternoon and told never to come back or have any contact with the girls—because if I did, I'd face legal action."

She cleared her throat. "And that was that. My bags were packed for me and I was escorted out without ever having a chance to say goodbye. I've never spoken to the twins or either parent since, and of course never used the Washburns as a reference, either. But some good did come of the situa-tion." She paused, looking both Dan and Walt in the eye. "It made me realize how much I wanted and needed a family of my own, so I decided to go it alone, I selected a sperm bank and, well, you know the rest...."

"I'M SORRY," DAN TOLD Emily after Walt had left. "I never would have permitted Walt to waylay you like that had I an inkling what he had up his sleeve."

More relieved now than upset, Emily shrugged. It felt good not to have this secret between them anymore. Truth be told, she didn't want to have *any* secrets between them. And not just because it made life so much easier, but because she wanted Dan to understand why she was going to have to quit. Sooner, rather than later. Emily forced a smile and slipped into a chair. Although the pregnancy fatigue was beginning to let up a bit in her second trimester, at times like this she still felt physically drained.

"If it's anyone's fault, it's mine. I just should've leveled with you from the start," Emily admitted, smoothing the hem of her black wool maternity skirt and crossing her legs at the knee. Taking a deep breath, she continued, "But I didn't because I figured what happened with the Washburn family really didn't apply to the situation since I was only going to be with you a very short time."

Dan looked at her, and once again Emily felt the electricity crackle between them. He looked a little taken aback, too. Maybe because this seemed to happen every time they were alone together. "I wish you'd given me more credit," he told her quietly.

Emily did, too. And yet she knew, given that the two of them were on such different life paths, it was best they not get too intimately involved with each other. Dan had his hands full running his architectural firm and parenting the three kids he already had. He didn't need to take on any of her concerns, nor did she need to take on his.

"Not that it matters, in any case," she blurted before she could stop herself.

Dan arched a brow.

Emily met Dan's calmly assessing gaze. "I'm pretty sure I'm going to go into partnership with Tex Ostrander."

Dan sat on the edge of his desk and faced her. Concern glimmered in his eyes. "What happened to your reservations?"

"They're still there," she confessed with shrug. "I know Tex'll try to run roughshod over me."

Dan's gaze narrowed. "And yet you're still willing to go into business with him."

Emily's hand dropped to her tummy. Her palm curved tenderly over the baby growing inside her. "I've got to do what is best for my baby," she said softly. And what was best, Emily knew, was carving out a legacy for her child's future.

DAN KNEW IT WAS A MISTAKE for Emily to ignore her instincts, which initially had been to say no to everything her ex-fiancé proposed. He also knew it wasn't his place to advise her on her career objectives.

Not at this stage of the game, anyway. So instead, he said, "If there is anything I can do…"

"Actually there is," Emily said with a smile, standing once again. She remained directly in front of him, her body braced in challenge. His heartbeat kicked up a notch. "Tex wants to gut the inside of the house I grew up in and turn it into a tearoom, and convert the barn on the property into a retail store. He thinks it will be cheaper than tearing down and starting anew. Before I agree to anything I'd like to get a second opinion. And since you're an architect…" She paused. "I figured maybe you'd know someone reputable in the Fredericksburg area I could contact to take a look at the property."

Finally seeing a way he could help, Dan offered, "*I* could do that for you."

Her high-sculpted cheeks glowed pink against the fairness of her complexion. Her dark silky hair fell in a straight blanket, brushing her shoulders. She rocked forward in her suede shoes. "But you're so busy…"

Dan tried not to recall how much he had enjoyed kissing those soft lips. Or how sweet and feminine her body had felt pressed against his. Even now, he fought the urge to hold her in his arms again…. "So are you," he countered implacably as he pushed his mind back to business, "and you found time to help me out when I needed it."

Again, that slight hesitation. She pressed her lips together, then said, "I'm not sure I could afford your rates."

Dan wasn't sure he could bear to walk away from her and the tantalizing image of what they might one day have, once all the barriers were dispensed with. "How about we barter, then?" he asked casually.

Her blue eyes glittered. "I'm listening."

He shifted forward enough to inhale the soft, womanly fragrance of her hair and skin. "You stay on as personal chef through Thanksgiving weekend—at the salary we've already agreed on. And this is *especially* important—I want you to make our holiday meal and dine with us." His lips quirked. "If you agree to my terms, I'll go with you to Fredericksburg. See the property, give you my honest opinion and draw up any plans you want."

She stepped back slightly. "When would we go?"

Dan mentally reviewed his schedule. "Saturday at noon okay with you?"

"You've got a deal. In the meantime, I'd better get going if you all are going to have dinner ready at six tonight." Emily started for her coat, scarf and shoulder bag.

"Emily—"

She turned.

"Thanks for everything," Dan said softly. "Being so honest in your assessment of my kids and helping us out."

Emily picked up her coat and put it over her arm. "It's my pleasure— Oh!" The garment slipped out of her fingers and fell to the floor.

But, Dan noted, she didn't look as if she was in pain. Just some sort of…shock. He looked at her closely in an effort to diagnose the problem. "Emily?"

She still didn't move. Didn't blink. Barely seemed to breathe.

Dan tensed in alarm. "Is everything okay?"

Chapter Six

Emily stood motionless, hardly able to believe… And then she felt it again. The tiniest movement, a fluttering deep inside. Her breath caught and moisture filled her eyes.

Dan's hand was on her arm, lightly touching, prompting. "Emily?" he said again. "What's wrong?"

The tears she'd been holding back spilled from her lashes and rolled down her cheeks. And still Emily couldn't move, couldn't bring herself to speak. And then…there it was again—the slight fluttering of life. Wanting to hang on to the sensation, this tiny baby she already loved so very much, she shut her eyes and savored the sheer exhilaration of the experience.

"Emily?" Dan tried again. "What is it?"

The tenderness in his voice made her meet his gaze. The warmth in his eyes held her rooted in place. She sucked in a breath, her throat too thick with tears for her to speak. She took his free hand and placed it on her lower abdomen, holding it firmly against her. And there it was again, the push against her skin from deep inside. An unbearable tenderness soared through her. More tears welled and coursed down her cheeks.

Dan finally understood and a smile as radiant as any she had ever seen spread across his face. "The baby," he murmured, shared joy sparkling in his eyes.

Emily nodded, feeling the love only a parent knew. Together, they stood absolutely still. Waiting. Waiting. And…nothing! It seemed, Emily realized with regret, that the tiny "Hello there!" was over.

Dan wrapped a reassuring arm about her shoulders. "Was that the first time you felt the baby move?"

Emily nodded, embarrassed to find she was still ridiculously choked up from the overwhelming proof that there really was life growing inside her. All she knew was that the sob of sheer joy that had been lodged in her throat made its way to her mouth. She was crying so hard she was shaking. Dan enfolded her in his arms. As he held her, she leaned into him, accepting his warmth and strength. And still, it seemed, she could not stop the flow of tears. Could not resist the soothing feel of his hand moving up and down her spine, or the soft words of comfort he murmured in her ear.

"I'm s-s-sorry," she said finally, trying hard to get it together. And failing.

Dan slid his hand beneath her chin and lifted her face to his. An abundance of emotion flowed between them. Her heart thumped and skittered and filled. "It's okay," he told her. "You've got every right. And look at *me*." He laughed. "I'm a little misty, too."

It was true. He was.

Her voice trembling as much as the rest of her, she forced out, "It's just…"

Dan looked deep into her eyes and finished for her, "A miracle."

"As much as I tried," Emily said, "I couldn't imagine…"

He nodded, touched. "I know."

"The first time I heard the baby's heartbeat in the doctor's office was something, too."

"Really gets you—" Dan's voice was rusty as he thumped his fist over his heart "—right here."

"Yes," Emily said. And then the blissful tears started again, flowing even faster this time.

Dan smiled and wiped the pad of his thumb across her cheek, stopping the flow of salty liquid making its way to her mouth. Emily gazed up at him with her lips parted. His head lowered, and then they were kissing again.

Yearning swept through her, as vital and real as the life growing within her. Dan flattened a hand over her spine, bringing her flush against him. They were touching from shoulder to knee. Giving in to the passion coursing through both of them, she wreathed her arms about his broad shoulders and went up on tiptoe. And still the need swept them along, the happiness brought about by her baby mixing with the reality of discovering this—

Had there not been a sudden, insistent buzzing of the phone on Dan's desk, who knew what might have happened? Emily thought as they reluctantly moved apart. With a look of acute disappointment, Dan let her go and went back to reach across his desk for the receiver. "Yes?" He listened. "No. Tell them not to disband. I'll be right there."

He replaced the receiver. "I've got to get back to my meeting."

Embarrassed, Emily looked around for her bag and slipped it back onto her shoulder. She ducked her head. "And I've got to get to work."

Dan caught her hand before she could reach the door. "We will talk about this," he promised softly.

Which was exactly what Emily most feared. An examination of feelings almost too complex to be borne. "Or not," she said with an equally determined smile. Still tingling from the kiss, she rushed off.

EMILY WALKED INTO THE Kingsland family kitchen from the back door, at the same time Ava dragged herself in from the other direction. The pretty teen tossed her backpack of books onto the kitchen table, where it landed with a hard thump, struggled out of her trendy suede jacket and threw it down, too. "I'm going to die!" she moaned, pressing her hand to the center of her forehead.

Emily had no experience with teenagers. But she knew how to take care of someone who was sick. She edged closer, taking in Ava's pallor and the beads of sweat on her forehead. "Do you think you have a fever?"

Ava shrugged listlessly. Tears gathered in her eyes. "All I know is my head is killing me. I have the worst headache ever!"

Emily risked the teen's wrath. She pressed the back of her knuckles lightly against Ava's cheek. Her temperature appeared normal. "Did you have coffee today?" she asked gently.

"No. I mean, I could have. Dad didn't forbid me to have any more caffeine, but he made me feel like it was so unhealthy—" she grimaced "—I had a caffeine-free soda instead, and have been so drowsy all day I don't think I heard a thing any of my teachers said. And then, to top it off, I got this headache!"

"Where do you keep the acetaminophen or aspirin?" Emily asked.

"In the cupboard above the fridge." Ava dragged herself into a chair and laid her head on the table. "Top shelf."

Emily got out the step stool. Found what she needed and shook out two pills. She took that and a glass of water over to Ava. "Take these. It'll help."

"I doubt it," Ava mumbled, but she complied.

"I think you have a caffeine-withdrawal headache," Emily said gently.

"That's what my friend said," Ava grumbled. "She told me to stop and get an espresso after school, but at that point just the idea made me so nauseous…"

"How about a big glass of lemon water and a snack instead?"

Ava looked desperate enough to try anything. "Sure. If you think it will help."

"I do. You know, I had a caffeine addiction myself when I was just a little older than you."

Ava's mouth quirked up. "I'm guessing you kicked it."

"Had to. I was a prep chef in a restaurant at the time and I was getting the jitters." Emily made a face as she worked, remembering. "Not a good thing to have when you're working with very sharp knives."

"I guess not." Ava lifted her head off the tabletop and sat up.

Emily set a plate of grapes, strawberries and apple slices in front of her. Slices of sharp white cheddar and a fan of soda crackers decorated the edge.

"So what'd you do?" Ava asked, munching on a cracker.

Finding she was a little hungry, too, Emily fixed herself a small plate and sat opposite the teen. "I quit cold turkey, and I'll be honest, I was pretty miserable for a couple of days with the same symptoms you're having, but once I got past that, life got a lot easier. I was able to wake up quicker in the morning, stopped having trouble staying awake in the afternoon and falling asleep at night. And then, of course, I learned all the ways to keep my blood sugar even and my energy level high."

The color coming back into her cheeks, Ava asked, "Will you teach me?"

Emily smiled. "I'd love to," she said.

FOR A MOMENT, DAN THOUGHT he'd come home to the wrong house. It wasn't just the autumn wreath on the front door and the vase of flowers on the console in the front hall. Or even the delicious smells coming from the kitchen. It was the sound of music and the ripple of female laughter.

Walt came in right behind Dan.

Brow furrowed, he muttered, "What the…?"

Dan shrugged. "Beats me." But he was determined to find out.

He set his briefcase down and shrugged out of his jacket, looping it over the banister, then headed for the rear of the house with Walt right behind him.

He stopped at what he saw.

Emily, Ava and Kayla were dancing up a storm in the middle of the kitchen. The lively rock music was turned up so loud and they were having so much fun, they had no idea they had an audience.

Until the back door opened and Tommy strode in, athletic bag slung over his shoulder. He, too, looked incredibly upbeat. Cell phone in hand, he was grinning from ear to ear. "Hey! Did you all get Mom's text message? She's coming home week after next, and she said we're all going to be together for an old-fashioned Thanksgiving!"

The girls stopped what they were doing.

Emily stepped forward and switched off the music.

The sudden absence of sound left them all staring at one another in shock.

"I thought she wasn't coming home until Christmas!" Ava said.

"Does this mean she won't be here for Christmas?" Kayla wailed.

Dan had no clue, so he answered as positively as possible. "I'm sure she wants to be," he said.

Ava tilted her head to one side. "Did Mom say anything to you about this?" she asked her father.

"We talked briefly earlier today," Dan admitted, realizing too late he probably should have mentioned that conversation to Emily when he insisted she be a part of their holiday celebration, as both handsomely compensated head chef and guest.

As it was, she was no doubt as blindsided by the news of Brenda's expedited homecoming as his kids were.

"And so what else did she say?" Tommy prodded impatiently as everyone waited.

Dan forced himself to be as cheerful as the situation required. "Your mom said what the text indicated. That she wants us to be together for the Thanksgiving holiday." For the first time in three years.

"I'm going to draw her a picture right now!" Kayla raced off, beside herself with excitement.

"I'm going to try and text her back!" Ava said.

"She's probably not going to be able to get it," Tommy cautioned her. "Mom said she's headed off into the wilds again, but I'm with you—let's try anyway!"

Ava nodded, for once completely in tune with her younger brother. "She'll get it eventually."

"If dinner is almost ready, I'd better wash up." Walt strode off, too.

Then, abruptly, only Emily and Dan remained.

"I have just one question," Emily said quietly, the depth of her disappointment vibrating between them. "When were you planning to tell me that I was going to be having dinner with you and your ex?"

DAN NEVER HAD A CHANCE to answer that question because Kayla was back, paper and crayons in tow. The actual dinner was equally fraught with excited chatter as plans were made for their mom's unexpectedly early visit.

Then Ava needed help with her physics homework.

Before Dan knew it, Emily had finished cleaning up and left for the evening. So he did what needed to be done to make sure his kids were all set for the evening, told Walt he needed to run an errand and drove to Emily's place. She opened the door, looking none too happy to see him there and not at all inclined to invite him in.

This was going to be harder than he expected. He took in the pushed-up sleeves of her V-neck sweater, fuzzy-slipper-clad feet and her carelessly upswept hair. "First of all—" he looked her squarely in the eye "—I want to thank you for the wreath on the front door."

"I picked it up at the farmers' market on impulse." Her tone was cool.

Dan worked to make peace. "It looks nice. Homey."

To no avail. She simply stood there, one hand planted against the frame, her outstretched arm blocking his way.

"I bought the autumn flowers, too. So..." Emily lifted her shoulders in an indifferent shrug "—if that's all..."

Dan had the feeling he wasn't being pushed away momentarily, but for good. The notion was disturbing, especially after the closeness they'd shared this afternoon. "About Thanksgiving...I'd like to explain."

Noting a man coming down the hall, artist's portfolio in one hand, a bundle of mail in the other, Emily frowned and gestured Dan in. Thankful for the timely entrance of what was obviously one of her neighbors, Dan followed and shut the door behind him.

"What's to explain?" Emily asked, striding to an open packing box sitting next to the bookshelf crammed with all manner of cookbooks. "I'm a temporary family employee. All I need to know is the number of guests and what type of menu you'd like for any given occasion. Along with any special dietary needs..."

Dan moved closer. "Cut the act. I know you're upset and you have every right to be. Uh...you probably should not be packing up these books in your condition."

Emily crossed her arms. In the soft light of her loft, she looked even more beautiful. "Notice I'm not actually lifting any of the book boxes."

Dan studied the determined tilt of her chin. "Yet."

She flushed.

Guilty as charged, Dan thought.

A roll of tape in her hand, she knelt, a feat that wasn't all that easy, given the figure-hugging cut of her black wool skirt. "Just say what you have to say, Dan."

He held the edges of the box together for her. He sensed he didn't have much time before she booted him out, so he went straight for the bottom line. "There's no reason for you to be jealous."

She dispensed the tape with a ripping sound, patted it none too gently in place, then slowly stood up. He did the same.

"What did you say?" she demanded indignantly.

Exasperated, Dan replied, "That there's no rea—"

The soft press of her index finger against his lips made him stop.

"I'm. Not. Jealous." She enunciated the words.

But she certainly looked it at this moment, Dan noted with a satisfaction that was distinctly male.

"Confused, perhaps," Emily said, dropping her hand.

His lips still tingling from her touch, Dan caught her fingers in his. Confused? "About what?"

She looked down at their intertwined hands, swallowed and said softly, "Why you felt the need to keep it from me."

Dan knew how it looked, but there had been nothing disingenuous about his actions. The truth was, whenever he was around Emily, it was hard to think of anything but her.

"I wasn't doing that," he argued.

To his frustration, her defenses remained firmly in place. Her gaze mocked him. "Really."

"Yes. I was focused on other things at the time," he told her, his eyes still locked with hers.

Emily released a slow, deliberate breath. "Like kissing me?"

A wistful feeling swept through Dan. Suddenly he wanted everything to be different. Starting with the boundaries they had tried to erect between them. "Like…everything about you," he said quietly. He watched as her irises darkened. "The way your hair gleams in certain lights. The softness of your lips. The vulnerability in your eyes and the maternal happiness you radiate. You are so beautiful, Emily." He didn't think she had any idea. "So incredibly, remarkably beautiful that when I'm with you, I can only think of one thing, and that's doing everything I can to make you happy."

He gathered her close. Feeling her melt against him, he kissed her cheek, her temple, the shell of her ear. Intoxicated with the sweet, silky feel of her once again, he inhaled the delicate blend of perfume and woman. Their lips touched in a tender kiss.

"This isn't sensible," Emily said, splaying her hands across his chest.

"Forget sensible," he told her gruffly, as astonished as she appeared to be by the way he was putting himself out there, allowing himself to hope that second chances might actually be possible. "And just be grateful instead," he persuaded her softly. "Grateful that we found each other. Grateful that it might not be too late for either of us to get what we want in this life. Grateful for all the days and weeks and months ahead."

Emily had told herself she wouldn't fall into the trap of being with a man just because she was at a point in her life where she did not want to be alone. She'd told herself that wanting each other desperately wasn't enough of a reason for two people to be together. In her heart of hearts, she knew there should be more than just desire and affection. There should be love and shared ideals and the kind of commitment that would last a lifetime. She and Dan did not have that, might never have all that, and yet…it was so easy to believe that after sharing a few hot kisses and the experience of having her baby move inside her, they just might have a shot at something special.

Dan was certainly everything she could ever have hoped the man in her life would be. Tall and handsome. Smart. Kind. The type of man who would do anything for his kids—and for her.

"Emily…Emily…" He buried his face in her hair and a ragged sigh escaped his lips. "You're going to have to tell me to leave."

Now, she ordered herself sternly, before it's too late. But even as the thought occurred, she knew she couldn't. She had been alone too long. Without comfort and closeness and the exhilarating completion of physical intimacy. She wanted him. She wanted this.

So instead, she pressed a kiss to his collarbone, took him by the hand and led him toward her bed. "Not," Emily said softly, looking deep into Dan's eyes, "before we do this."

DAN KNEW AS WELL AS Emily did all the reasons the two of them shouldn't be together. But damned if he could think of a single one as she sat on the edge of the bed, looked at him expectantly and kicked off her slippers.

His pulse racing as out of control as his heart, Dan knelt before her and pressed a kiss to her knee. She shuddered with reaction. Hands encircling her waist, he brought her hips to the very edge of the bed. Her skirt rode high on her thighs. Wanting to please her, he parted her knees and slipped his hands between them.

The air was thick with lust and the harsh sounds of their breathing.

Emily wrapped her arms around his neck and leaned forward so they could kiss again, and kiss they did. Slowly, patiently, softly, hotly. Dan's body throbbed as he eased a hand beneath her sweater. He caressed her through the fabric of her bra, the fullness of her breasts filling his hands, the tautness of her nipples pushing against his palm. Need spiraled through him. Trembling with passion, Emily reached for the hem of her sweater, lifted it high above her head.

Her bra was black satin and lace that, thanks to a swiftly unhooked back clasp, soon went the way of the sweater. He hadn't been this turned-on...well, ever. "Lovely," he murmured.

"The veins..." Emily ducked her head self-consciously and touched the bluish lines running across her pregnancy-full breasts.

"They're perfect, too," Dan said, never meaning anything more, and to prove it, kissed everywhere he'd touched. Caressed and stroked. When her back arched and she moaned, he moved down the curve of her belly to the elastic insert at the top of her maternity skirt.

"I suppose," Emily said breathlessly, lifting slightly to allow him free rein, "this has to come off, too."

"Most definitely." Aware he'd never wanted to possess a woman more, Dan eased it off, then followed with tights and panties.

"This feels...awkward," Emily whispered as he kissed his way from her navel to her knee. Her cheeks blushed a pretty pink as she looked at him with the same overwhelming need he felt. "I've never..."

"Made love as a pregnant woman," Dan guessed, liking the excited glitter in her eyes.

Emily nodded, her breath coming erratically.

"Then," Dan said, kissing her thoroughly before moving lower still, "you're in for a treat."

DAN HADN'T BEEN KIDDING, Emily thought dizzy moments later as he slowly disrobed and joined her on the bed, pulling her back into his arms. Pregnancy hormones amplified everything and his sensual expertise brought forth even more. "You are so right," she whispered.

Common sense told her they wouldn't be doing this again. But for now…

What was one night, one moment in time, except something to be grateful for? And she was grateful for the feel of his strong arms around her as he guided her onto her back and stretched out beside her. One arm sliding beneath her shoulders, he lifted her head to his. The kiss drew them closer still. She explored his body as wantonly as he had explored hers. And then they were shifting again, he was bracing his weight on his arms and draping his body over hers. Inundated with the masculine warmth of him, she put her arms about his neck and opened herself to him. To the sensation of being taken, and the knowledge she was taking in return. To the feel of being one with him. To the idea that family was not completely out of reach. And then all was lost in the heat and intensity of the moment, of the rushing adrenaline and the thrill of the pleasure that spiraled out of control and morphed into sweet, hot satisfaction.

For long moments after, they lay like that, bodies shuddering and intimately entwined, his weight still braced on his arms.

With her eyes shut, Emily savored the closeness. It had been so long since she had been held. So long since she had felt so much a woman, so wanted. So long since she had dared hope—

And of course that was when Dan's cell phone went off,

the chime breaking the silence of the room. That was all it took to dispel the sensual, carefree mood.

Dan tensed. A second later, he carefully disengaged their bodies. Reached down beside the bed and removed the cell phone from his belt. He glanced at the screen and relaxed slightly. "That was a text message from Walt. He said Ava is upstairs studying, and Tommy's working out one last time before bed. Kayla is asleep…and he's going to bed himself."

Dan texted back, then put the phone aside. Looking completely relaxed, albeit slightly distracted, he rolled onto his side and propped his head on his upraised hand. Feeling a bit guilty for keeping him from his kids, Emily said, "If you want to leave…"

Dan shook his head. "No. That's the last thing I want." He wrapped a strand of her hair around his fingertip. "This is the first time in years I've lost track of the fact I've got kids at home and the responsibility that goes with them. To be honest, I'd forgotten what it felt like to be with someone this way."

Emily had *never* known what it was like to be with someone this way. To feel that nothing mattered but being in Dan's arms, receiving and returning his kiss. He'd opened up a whole new world of wanting to her tonight.

"You must be looking forward to the empty nest every-one talks about," she suggested.

Dan's lips quirked into a wistful smile. "I have to admit there are times when the thought of being able to do what I want, when I want, sounds pretty appealing."

His longing hit home. Emily wanted to look out for his best interests the way he had unselfishly looked out for hers. "Which is maybe why," Emily supposed softly, trying to be cautious, for both their sakes, "we shouldn't let this go any further."

Dan's brows drew together.

Emily rose, wrapping the sheet around her. She disappeared into the bathroom and came back in a white, terrycloth spa robe. She sat on the edge of the bed beside him, her natural practicality taking over. "You've carried the never-ending responsibility of fatherhood for eighteen years now." *And you're already looking forward to regaining your freedom.* "I'm just getting started with the whole parenthood thing."

His eyes darkened and he captured her hand with his. "That doesn't mean…"

She stopped him with a smile meant to let him off the hook. "I know you're a stand-up guy—"

"Who isn't into one-night stands any more than you are," Dan interjected gruffly.

Emily nodded and forged on. "And because of that…because you're so decent and honorable, because we've both been alone for so long, we're both going to be tempted to make this more than it is." She placed her finger on his lips before he could interrupt again. "I'm telling you, you don't have to do that." She paused, letting her words sink in. Nervously she traced the seam on the belt of her robe. "I'm letting you off the hook."

He studied her inscrutably, silent now. "You want to pretend this never happened," he said finally.

Realistically? Now that the hormonal need to be with someone had ebbed? Emily didn't see it any other way. "You and I both know that what happened between us was mostly due to the fact I'm pregnant…and alone." *And on the brink of falling hard for you.* Emily swallowed.

"Hormones aren't a basis for a relationship." Nor was what had happened earlier that day.

"Today...in my office..." Dan started.

Emily lifted her hand. "There's no denying that was a truly magical moment. It would be for any two people who happened to find themselves together in that particular circumstance."

Dan remained unconvinced.

"I'm really happy you were there to share the moment with me when I first felt my baby move." Okay, now she was babbling.

Dan studied her, his emotions now as tightly wrapped and hidden from view as her own. "So am I," he said warily.

"And that lent an intimacy to our relationship that would not otherwise have been there. Had it not happened, I would've walked out at the end of our conversation. And that would've been that. There would've been no embrace, no second kiss. And certainly no lovemaking tonight."

Once again Dan was silent. He rubbed the flat of his hand across his jaw, looking suddenly so much older than his years. "What do you want to do?' he asked eventually.

Be with you again, Emily thought, without complication or consequence or thought to the future. But she knew she couldn't do that. She would soon be a parent. Just like Dan. She had to be responsible. To her baby, to Dan. And what he needed was not what she had to give.

Her throat tight, she forced herself to do the right thing and say, "I think we should go back to being employer and employee."

And if they were lucky, she mused dispiritedly, perhaps even friends.

Chapter Seven

Dan wasn't sure what he expected when he came in from work Wednesday evening. Certainly not family togetherness.

Ava had her homework and AP textbooks spread out over the kitchen table. A tall glass of ice water and fruit plate next to her, she had her headphones and iPod on and seemed to be studying intently. Through the big kitchen windows, Dan saw that Tommy was outside on the back deck, still in his wrestling-practice clothes, talking on the cordless phone. Walt was outside, too, arranging the wood that had just been delivered into manageable stacks. Emily, in a burgundy chef's smock and trim black pants, had her head bent next to Kayla's as the two pored over a cookbook. The tableau before him made his heart skip a beat.

How long had it been, he wondered, since the members of his family had come together without being forced to do so?

How long since he'd felt the jolt of sweet and tender awareness he experienced every time he laid eyes on Emily?

How long had he been able to go today without remembering how great it had been to make love with her?

And yet, he reminded himself soberly, Emily had made it clear that their lovemaking the night before had been a one-time-only thing. A fling that needed to be appreciated for what it was and then promptly forgotten…if he wanted her to continue working in his home.

"Daddy, we're going to make our own pizzas tonight, and then after dinner we're going to make corn bread," Kayla explained.

Dan looked at the big bowl of salad sitting on the counter and the bowls of toppings, ready to go on six individual-size pizza doughs.

Tommy came in through the back door and set the receiver on the hook. "Some lady from the elementary school called," he announced cheerfully. "You're confirmed for tomorrow, Dad."

Dan blinked. "Confirmed for what?"

"Making corn bread stuffing with me!" Kayla announced.

Frowning at Dan's blank look, Ava took off her headphones. "It's the Thanksgiving feast, Dad," she said, exasperated. "The third-graders get together and make turkey and stuff, and then sit down with their parents and eat together. They do it every year."

"Usually the week before Thanksgiving," Tommy chimed in.

Embarrassed to feel so clueless when it came to his kids, Dan shook his head. "I don't remember that."

"That's 'cause you weren't there when I was in third grade," Ava said matter-of-factly. "Mom was—or she was supposed to be until she had some emergency come up at the hospital."

Tommy studied the pizza fixings, then chowed down on a thin slice of green pepper. "No one was there for me, either," he said. "But all the other kids had their parents there."

Guilt stung Dan. Life had been completely chaotic during those years of his marriage to Brenda. Two careers going full force, no one really minding the store at home. The kids had survived, but they'd been hurt.

With a glance that was equal parts sympathy and censure, Emily plucked a piece of paper off the counter. She handed it to Dan, looked him straight in the eye and brought him up to speed. "Kayla's teacher sent this reminder home with her. You're supposed to show up at school tomorrow morning at nine, with two thirteen-by-nine pans of corn bread and the rest of the ingredients for the stuffing."

"And then you teach the kids in your group how to make it and let them help," Ava said. "Pretty simple stuff."

For an ace in the kitchen, Dan thought. He had his hands full trying to follow the directions on a store-bought frozen dinner.

"What's the matter, Daddy?" Kayla wrinkled her nose.

"I'm not sure I can be there on such short notice," Dan admitted reluctantly.

Kayla's face fell. Her lower lip trembled and she looked ready to burst into tears.

"I can go in your place, if you like," Emily offered.

Their eyes met, held. Dan wasn't sure how he felt about the bailout. Relieved or unfairly spared. He only knew he was glad Emily was there.

Emily put an arm around Kayla's shoulders. "I'm very good at teaching people how to cook," she said.

Kayla glared at her father, then turned to Emily, wrapped her arms around Emily's middle and buried her head against Emily's chest. "I'd like that very much," she said.

EMILY WALKED INTO THE Fort Worth elementary school cafeteria, where bedlam reigned even without the third-grade students in attendance. In the midst of all the women running to and fro setting up the early-morning cooking activity stood a lone man. In a forest-green dress shirt and black slacks, Dan stood uncertainly off to one side. He held a folded-up white apron and wore a mildly confused expression.

Emily hurried toward him as quickly as the box in her arms would allow.

Seeing her, Dan dropped the apron on the table marked Kingsland/Corn bread. "Let me help you with that." He rushed forward.

Their forearms brushed as the transfer was made. "I didn't think you were going to make it this morning," Emily said, tingling at the contact and catching a whiff of his crisp aftershave.

Emily tore her eyes away from the just-shampooed softness of his sandy-blond hair. He'd shaved, too—in the bright morning sunlight flooding through the windows, she could see just how close.

Dan set the box down on the table. "I talked to my clients. Fortunately they were understanding—that isn't always the case—and agreed to reschedule their session with me for this evening."

Emily set the ingredients on the table. "Kayla's going to be really happy."

"I don't know. She was still pretty mad at me this morning."

Finished, Emily rocked back on her heels. Her glance was compassionate. "You didn't know."

Dan exhaled. "I should have."

Nothing she could say to that. It was true. They stared at each other in silence.

The mom in charge came by. She looked at Dan and Emily. "Which of you is making the corn-bread stuffing with the kids?"

"We both are," Dan said, extending a hand. "I'm Dan Kingsland. This is Emily Stayton. I've never made stuffing. She has. So she'll be doing the teaching."

"Great. Glad to have you both." The mom looked at Emily's trim black skirt and green sweater. "Cute, the way you dressed alike, too."

Emily blushed. She'd been so busy looking at Dan and enjoying his company she hadn't noticed. "Completely accidental, I assure you," she murmured.

The mom laughed. "Great minds think alike, hmm?" she said. She hurried off, tossing her departing words over her shoulder. "I'll see what I can do about finding another apron!"

Dan winked at Emily. "If our matching attire embarrasses you, I could go home and change."

Emily's cheeks warmed all the more. "And miss a single second of this gala?" she teased back, determined to hold her own with him. "Not a chance."

Their eyes held again. As the moment drew out and awareness grew, she thought about the night they'd made love, the pleasure they'd both felt, the warmth and tenderness he'd shown her. If only their lives weren't on such different paths, she thought wistfully. But they were, so there was no use pretending they were anything more than boss/employee.

She pulled her gaze away and began rearranging the ingredients on the table.

Obviously perplexed by the abrupt dampening of her mood, Dan plucked his apron off the table and handed it to her. "In case they don't have extra, you can have this one."

Glad to have something else besides the ingredients and his sexy presence to focus on, Emily unfolded the white cotton. "I have a feeling you're going to need it more than me."

His eyes lit up at the teasing jab. "Ha-ha."

She motioned for him to bend down so she could slip the loop over his head. Because he still seemed a little clueless, she straightened the fabric, then grabbed the ties and stepped behind him. "At least you look professional," she joked.

He chuckled and sensual electricity arced through her.

"Careful," he warned with a playful lift of his brows. "I just might show you up."

"That'll be the day," Emily joked back. Although, given the skill he'd shown just about everywhere else, especially in the bedroom…

"Daddy!" Kayla's exuberant voice had them turning in unison.

The eight-year-old barreled into Dan's arms. "I didn't think you were going to come!"

He hugged his daughter tight.

"And Emily, too!" Kayla reached over and grabbed Emily, bringing the three of them into a group hug. Emily's eyes met Dan's over Kayla's head. *This is what it must feel like to be part of a complete family,* she thought.

When she'd decided to become pregnant, she hadn't felt she needed a conventional family to find the happiness she'd been yearning for. She'd thought a baby alone would do it. Now she couldn't help but wonder. Had she been wrong?

After a few moments, Kayla ended the embrace. She

jumped up and down, exclaiming, "Emily, I told my teacher we made the corn bread together last night!"

Kayla's teacher waved all the students to the center of the cafeteria. "Whoops! I gotta go!" The little girl raced off.

Dan turned to Emily and observed dryly, "I think she might be excited."

Still feeling the warmth of the family hug, Emily smiled. "Just a little bit." *Kayla isn't the only one,* she thought.

LUCKILY FOR EMILY, she had plenty to keep her occupied the rest of the day. As did Dan. Hence it was with relief, or so she told herself, that they parted company immediately after the third-grade Thanksgiving feast.

For a change, Tommy was the first one home.

"Where's Dad?" Tommy asked, coming into the kitchen at five-fifteen and carrying his athletic bag.

Noting the teen looked like he needed his dad now, Emily delivered the bad news. "He's having dinner with a client."

Tommy grabbed the next available lifeline. "Uncle Walt?"

"Also meeting with a client. He won't be here for dinner tonight, either."

Tommy's shoulders slumped. She watched as he walked into the laundry room. Moments later she heard the washer rumble on. Then, as she was putting romaine lettuce into the salad spinner, he came back into the kitchen, sat down at the counter and buried his head in his hands.

Her heart going out to the dispirited boy, she asked, "Anything I can help you with?"

Tommy exhaled loudly. "Doubt it."

Emily handed Tommy a big glass of ice water. "Try me."

For a moment Emily didn't think Tommy would confide in her. Then he lifted his head and began to speak. "Friday night is our first official wrestling meet. We had a practice run. I lost my match and I shouldn't have. I'm better than that guy. But I just…I don't know… I ran out of steam at the end."

Emily had been waiting for a chance to talk to Tommy about his eating habits. "It must be hard, trying to stay a certain weight," she sympathized.

"Harder than I thought," Tommy lamented. He rubbed the back of his neck. "It's okay if you're underweight— you can always wrestle in a heavier class. But you can't *exceed* the weight you're supposed to wrestle at."

Emily leaned against the counter, listening. "How are you doing?"

"Actually I was two and a half pounds under today at the weigh-in," Tommy reported proudly.

"That's good."

"Yeah, I was relieved. Some of the guys were over their stated limit."

Which meant, Emily knew, they couldn't wrestle at all. Figuring it was now or never, Emily retrieved her shoulder bag and withdrew a stack of stapled papers she'd printed out. "You know your dad hired me to consult, as well as cook?"

Tommy nodded.

"Well, I was thinking about what I needed to do for you…. So since I don't know a lot about wrestling, I went to the website for the Olympic Training Center and got some information on what their athletes eat." She handed him the papers. "Take a look and see what you think, and then we'll figure out how to best handle your nutritional needs while you're competing."

EMILY WAS JUST GETTING ready for bed when Dan called that evening. "Hey," he said softly, "it's Dan."

She knew. Her consciousness had been imprinted with his voice long before they had ever foolishly made love. Feeling the baby kick, as if to say hello to Dan, too—she climbed into bed. Relaxing against the pillows, she put one hand on her tummy. "Everything okay?"

"Everything's great. Tommy's really happy about all the information you pulled together for him."

Emily warmed at Dan's praise. Trying hard not to think about the night Dan had lain here next to her, she turned her thoughts back to the business of helping his son. "Tommy will have a much easier time making weight if he sticks to the high-carbohydrate diet. Which brings me to the next point. I know you wanted everyone to be eating the same thing—and I can do that to a point—but with Tommy in training, he's going to need some adjustments to his evening meal that the others won't."

"That's fine. I primarily wanted everyone to come together, as a family, and that seems to be happening more and more each day."

"I've noticed the change, too." Emily paused, wishing they could continue to talk personal matters like this. But with the lines between them already hopelessly blurring, she knew it would be wiser to avoid temptation. She forced a brisk professional note into her voice. "Was there anything else?"

Dan cleared his throat. "Unfortunately, yes. I'm not going to be there for dinner tomorrow night, either, although Walt will be."

Emily quelled her disappointment. Wise or not, she had gotten used to seeing him most every evening. "Thanks for letting me know in advance." She forced herself to sound ultracasual. "Do you want me to leave a plate for you in the fridge?"

"If you wouldn't mind," he said just as casually, "that would be great."

Now it was her turn to deliver some not-so-terrific news. Emily took a deep breath. "I hate to do this, but I'm going to need both Friday and Saturday evenings off this week. I'm going down to Fredericksburg on Friday morning to meet with the attorney Tex hired to draft our partnership agreement."

Silence fell.

Emily wished she and Dan were face-to-face. She wanted to be able to look at his expression, see what he was thinking.

Finally Dan asked, in a voice that remained cautiously matter-of-fact, "Does this mean you've decided to go into business with him?"

Emily rubbed her hand over her tummy. "I'm still thinking about it. Considering all my options. But yes, I'm definitely leaning in that direction."

Dan cleared his throat. "Did you and Tex still want me to meet you there Saturday at noon?"

Emily envisioned seeing Dan on her old stomping grounds. Would that be more romantic—or less? Especially given that her ex-fiancé would be there with him. Aware she still hadn't answered Dan's question, she said, "Yes. I'll e-mail the directions to you."

Another pause, and this time Emily could have sworn she heard the reservation in Dan's voice. "I'll see you then."

SATURDAY DAWNED HUMID and cool, with heavy afternoon storms predicted for most of the state. Dan encountered no rain on the four-hour drive south, but the horizon was darkening ominously by the time he turned his luxury SUV into the lane that led to Emily's childhood home. She was already there waiting for him, sitting on the steps of the wide front porch of the small, white-stone ranch house.

Acutely aware he hadn't laid eyes on her in almost seventy-two hours, Dan cut the engine and got out. She was smiling from ear to ear, looking as at ease in the country as she did the city. She stood up and dusted off the back of her pants. "Glad you could make it," she said as she ambled down the steps.

She wore close-fitting jeans tucked into knee-high suede boots, a red, long-sleeved T-shirt that showed off the soft slope of her baby bump and a short denim jacket that no longer met in the middle. Her hair was loose and wavy, her cheeks pink.

Telling himself not to get too excited—this was a business trip after all—Dan slung his camera around his neck and grabbed his notepad. "Tex here yet?" he asked.

Emily stood beside Dan. "He had to go to his orchard in the Rio Grande Valley. They're expecting a big freeze from that cold front moving our way. He's got to make sure his citrus crop is protected."

Dan tried not to look too happy about the man's absence.

Emily stuck her hands in the pockets of her jacket. "I thought we'd tour the house last. See the barn and orchard first."

"Sounds good."

Together they walked across a gravel drive and an unmanicured lawn to a large, white two-story barn. Weathered wood showed beneath the peeling paint. Inside, the cement floor was stained with motor oil, mud and what appeared to be the remains of spoiled fruit.

"I know." Emily sighed. "The previous owners did a lousy job of taking care of the place."

Dan got his camera out. Noting the barn had no electricity, he checked out the integrity of the structure—the place seemed solid—and took flash photos.

"We were thinking the house would eventually be a small restaurant or tearoom, which could be expanded if business proves good enough."

"Gotcha."

Emily gestured expansively at their surroundings. "And this barn would be a retail space."

"Two floors or one?" Dan asked.

"Two—if we can swing it financially," she said.

Dan nodded.

From there, they walked to the orchard. There were rows upon rows of trees. "My dad planted all twelve varieties of Texas peaches," Emily said. "The first crop was ready in early May, the last in early August."

"So you had fruit…"

"For nearly four months. If we were to eventually farm tomatoes and apples, as Tex has suggested, we'd have crop to sell through October."

"That's great."

Emily led the way through the weed-choked aisles. "A lot of these trees are in really bad shape, though. They haven't been pruned in I don't know how long." Emily pivoted on her heel and stood facing Dan, her hands shoved in the back pockets of her jeans. Her posture only accentuated her baby bump—to Dan, she had never looked sexier.

Emily was frowning. "New trees should have been planted in the places where others were lost, but haven't been. Fortunately—" her serious blue gaze meshed with Dan's green one again "—it's nothing a lot of hard work won't fix."

He nodded and took some pictures of the rows of fruit trees, too. "Are peaches all that's grown here?"

"On this farm. Tex's folks expanded to include blackberries, strawberries, nectarines and plums, and he'd like to do the same over here, as well as add the aforementioned tomatoes and apples on the forty acres that aren't being farmed."

"So the orchards would go right up to the house and barn," Dan said.

Emily nodded, not looking happy about that. "Pretty much, yes. There'd be very little yard when all was said and done."

Or privacy, Dan thought. Especially if they turned the barn into a retail store.

Together, they headed back to the house. All around them, the wind was whipping up, pushing the hair into their eyes and plastering their clothes to their bodies. By the time they reached the front porch of the house, big fat drops of rain were falling.

Emily opened the door. Dan wasn't sure what he was expecting when she led the way inside.

Certainly not what he saw.

EMILY HIT THE LIGHTS, then turned to see the amazed look on Dan's face. Obviously he'd expected an empty home.

"Tex bought the place furnished."

Dan continued to look around. "I see why you wanted to buy it," he said, as impressed as she had been when she'd first laid eyes on the house again.

"It's perfect for a small family."

Emily showed him through the living room with its wide-plank oak floors, steeply angled ceiling and white-washed paneling. Built-in bookshelves flanked the white-stone fireplace. An overstuffed chintz sofa and chairs formed a conversation area in front of the fire, and floor-length draperies matched the upholstery. Behind the living room was a country kitchen, with wood floor, white cabinets, large farmhouse-style sink, stainless-steel appliances and marble countertops. An oak table accommodated four ladder-back chairs.

On the opposite side of the hall that ran front to back was a master bedroom with a four-poster bed and updated bath, complete with claw-foot tub and shower stall. A small nursery, decorated with a unisex pastel alphabet theme, was at the rear.

The place, which even had plantation shutters covering every window, was absolutely gorgeous and move-in ready. All she had needed to bring for her weekend stay were clothes and food. Everything else, down to the linens and dishes, was already here.

Dan continued to look around as they made their way past the laundry closet and into the kitchen. He shook his head, baffled. "It's hard to reconcile this with the condition of the rest of the property," he said.

Emily nodded, unable to mask her disappointment about that. "They really let the orchards and barn go."

"You had planned to live here."

Emily nodded. "I'd hoped to close on the property and be living here in my childhood home by Christmas." Sadness swept through her. "But it didn't work out…" She corralled her emotions with effort and moved past Dan, avoiding his assessing gaze. "Would you like some tea? I'm really…cold…for some reason."

"The temperature is dropping outside."

Emily paused in the act of reaching for the kettle. "Maybe I should build a fire first." She'd had one the night before and it had really warmed the house through and through, just as it had when she was a child.

Dan held up a staying hand. "Why don't you let me handle that," he said with a comforting smile that made her very glad he was here. He was, she decided as she set about completing the task, exactly the distraction she needed.

Chapter Eight

"You don't like this idea, either," Dan guessed four hours later.

Emily leaned against the kitchen counter, studying the image Dan had conjured up on his laptop computer screen. The rain was still pounding relentlessly on the roof. "It's not that it isn't a gorgeously imagined building," she said carefully.

Dan pushed back his chair and stood, too. "It's that you don't want to turn your childhood home into a restaurant."

Emily turned her glance to the kitchen window and gloomy landscape outside. "I know it has to be done," she said slowly. This was, after all, why he was here.

"You just can't bring yourself to start the process."

Emily began to pace. "The house is so beautiful just as it is, inside and out." When she had come to see it, before putting in a bid on the place, it had been so easy to see herself living here again, raising her child.

So easy to chase after old dreams.

She swallowed. "It seems a shame to destroy it. And that's what gutting the inside to add on a dining area and a commercial kitchen would do."

So don't, Dan's look said.

"On the other hand—" Emily forced herself to take a deep breath and be practical "—I know the orchards will attract a lot more business during busy season if we have an elegant tearoom and a retail store on-site. With the seed money Tex is willing to put into this venture, if we start now, we could have both up and running by the time the first crop of peaches ripens in mid-May."

Dan's brow furrowed. "Isn't that about the time you're due?"

Good point, Emily thought uneasily. One she hadn't really considered. "A month or so later. I'm due April tenth." She studied his suddenly poker-faced expression. "What?" she demanded impatiently.

He kept his eyes locked with hers. Said, with a great deal of sympathy, "I was just thinking that's a lot for anyone to handle alone."

Emily had heard that a lot since becoming pregnant. She just hadn't expected to hear it from him. She stiffened her spine and glared at Dan. "Thanks for the vote of confidence." She'd thought that Dan understood how very badly she wanted a family of her own, that he approved of her decision to become a single mother.

He spread his hands wide and gave her an understanding look. "I wasn't trying to be insulting."

Emily folded her arms in front of her, her temper spiking. "You succeeded admirably, nevertheless."

Dan smiled at her in the same indulgent way she had seen other men smile at their pregnant wives.

A mixture of wistfulness and pregnancy hormones combined, leaving her feeling all the more out of sorts. "*Now* what?" she asked.

Dan made no effort to hide the affection in his grin. "I was just thinking, we're having our first fight."

Unwanted emotion welled up inside her. "We are not!" she tossed back.

Dan's sexy grin widened. Laugh lines appeared at the corners of his eyes. "I think we are."

Indignant, Emily threw up her arms and sputtered, "To have a fight we'd—" Suddenly she couldn't go on.

"What?" he coaxed, coming close enough to lace his arms around her waist.

The warmth and strength of his body engulfed her, making it difficult to keep track of the argument she was trying to make. Harder still to fight the need for closeness. She drew a deep breath and tried again. "To have a fight we'd have to be…involved."

"Funny." Dan lowered his head and scored his thumb across her lower lip. "That's just what I was thinking."

A thrill soared through her. "Dan…"

He touched his lips lightly to hers in an angel-soft kiss. "Have I told you how much I like it when you catch your breath and look at me like that?" He kissed the side of her neck. "As if you can't help but want me as much as I want you? And I do want you, Emily," he told her in a low, gravelly voice, tangling his hands in her hair, bringing his lips closer still. "So much."

"I—" The rest of her sentence was cut off by a real kiss. Deeply passionate. Sensually evocative. And wonderfully, incredibly tender. A ribbon of desire went through Emily, followed swiftly by a torrent of need. The next thing she knew she was standing on tiptoe, pressing her body to Dan's. His hands drifted lower, sweeping up and down her spine, and still they kept on kissing, while the rain lashed the windows and drummed on the roof.

Emily heard herself moan, and then he was lifting her in his arms. Carrying her through the hall to the four-poster bed in the master.

He laid her down gently in the shadowy light.

And suddenly there was nothing else to say. Nothing but the need to feel his body stretched out along the length of hers. Quickly they undressed and slid beneath the sheets.

Dan pulled her back into his arms. His touch as hot and sensual as his kiss, he made his way down her body, taking his time. Caressing each curve, stopping to pay tender, reverent homage to the maternal slope of her tummy, before going lower still. Reveling in the intimate contact, Emily closed her eyes and gave herself over to him and the feelings gathering deep inside her.

She had made the baby inside her in the most scientific of ways, thinking that new life growing inside her was all she needed to make her life complete. Dan made her see things differently. He made her feel as if this baby was his, too, in ways that went beyond the facts to something far deeper and more wide-reaching. He made her feel as if a complete family was well within her reach. As if it was possible to give this baby she was carrying a daddy and a mommy. And a brother and sisters, too.

And that was a dangerous idea to have, she knew.

Yet she couldn't stop herself from having the fantasy any more than she could stop herself from responding in the here and now, she thought as their mouths fused in an explosion of heat and hunger. He laid claim to her, his tongue sweeping her mouth, his palms molding her breasts, his thumbs caressing the tender crests. And wise or not, she wanted to lose herself to him. She wanted the bliss and the intimacy only Dan could bring.

EMILY LAY WITH HER HEAD on Dan's chest, her legs tangled with his. She felt content to the point that if she'd had any common sense at all, it would have scared the heck out of her. But she didn't have any common sense. Not when she was alone with Dan. This afternoon had proved that.

The thought that she wanted many more times just like this was more disturbing still. She had become accustomed to being alone, to having no family but the child growing inside her.

Dan made her yearn for so much more.

And she could tell by the look in his eyes, sometimes, that he yearned, too. For a way to fill the empty spaces in his life and heal a family fractured by divorce.

He smoothed a hand through her hair, the movement enough to lull her to sleep. Or it would have been if not for the distinctive ring of her cell phone.

And that quickly, she knew who it was. And what he wanted to know. Once again, she couldn't believe she had let herself end up in such an untenable position.

DAN WAITED FOR EMILY to get off the phone with her future business partner. She walked back into the bedroom, a blanket wrapped around her, her cell phone still in her hand.

He was lying in bed with the sheet drawn to his waist and hands folded behind his head. "What did Tex say?"

Emily's eyes took on a troubled sheen as she related, "He was surprised I couldn't give him a detailed description of my plan for the proposed tearoom. He expected things to come together more quickly."

Tex Ostrander was being completely unreasonable, Dan thought. And pushy, to boot. "You just got started four hours ago," he said.

Emily stepped into the bathroom. When she came out, she was wrapped in a charcoal-gray terry robe. She dropped the soft cotton blanket on the foot of the bed and sat down beside it. Regretfully she met Dan's eyes. "My dad was always very quick to make things happen when it came to business. And Tex is an impatient man."

"Too impatient, it would seem," Dan said.

"Can't say I mind the interruption, though." Emily compressed her lips together. Regret laced her low tone. "The way I behaved this afternoon…is not at all like me. I don't get physically and emotionally involved with clients."

Dan had thought they were a lot more than personal chef and client. The fact that she never did this just proved it.

But sensing that now was not the time to bring that point up, he let his argument go and concentrated, instead, on bringing her what comfort he could from a business perspective. "Deciding whether to double the width or the depth of the building, or keep the footprint of the house as is and put on a second floor is a big decision."

Emily stood, restless again. "And one that must be made quickly if we are to proceed. The problem is—" she threw up her hands in frustration "—I can't seem to make it!"

It was all Dan could do to ignore his instincts and not take her in his arms again. Aware such a move was not likely to be well received, he stayed where he was. "Maybe you just need to take a break. We could go have dinner in town, relax for a bit, then get back at it."

"No." Emily tightened the belt of her robe. "The last thing we need is to sit across from each other in a candlelit room."

Dan could see how that could easily turn romantic. All they had to do was be near each other and look into each other's eyes to accomplish that. He shrugged. "So we'll go to a bar that's crowded and noisy." Whatever would help, he thought.

Emily pressed her lips together in that stubborn way he was beginning to know so well. "I don't want to end up getting sidetracked with you again." She gathered up her clothing and disappeared into the bathroom once more.

Knowing their lovemaking was over—for now, anyway—Dan rolled off the bed and took the opportunity to get dressed, too.

When Emily emerged from the bathroom, she had her clothes on and her hair brushed. She strode past him to the kitchen. "I'll cook dinner for us while we work."

As Dan watched the sexy play of her hips beneath her jeans, he realized a simple affair was never going to be enough. Not for him and not for Emily. To be happy, they both needed so much more than fleeting intimacy in their lives.

"You don't have to do that," Dan said.

She lifted a hand. "I had planned to cook for both you and Tex this evening anyway, and besides, it helps me think."

Willing to do anything to help her feel better, Dan took a seat in front of his laptop computer and sketch pad once again.

"The thing is," Emily said as she pulled ingredients for a traditional German meal from the fridge, "I could make food for a small tearoom in the kitchen I have right now, if I were offering a limited menu and doing it more or less on my own. Sandwiches and sweets are things that can be prepared in advance."

Dan watched her search the cupboards and pull out a large cast-iron skillet.

"We don't have a commercial cook space the way this kitchen is currently laid out. But we wouldn't need one for tearoom fare." Emily poured a little olive oil into the skillet.

"Seating would still be a problem," Dan thought out loud. "Unless you wanted to limit it to twelve or so customers at a time."

"I'm afraid if we did that, we'd lose more business than we'd gain. Customers coming out here to buy fruit aren't going to want to wait forty-five minutes for a table."

Dan picked up his sketch pad. "Will the retail store be open year-round or just in peach season?"

"Tex wants to ship fruit from his apple and citrus orchards in the Rio Grande Valley for sale here, as well. He'll make more money if he can cut out the middleman. And apples are in the fall, citrus in winter."

"So you'd be year-round," Dan surmised.

Emily nodded and slid German-style Texas smoked sausage into the pan.

"The climate here is temperate. You could always offer outdoor seating under umbrellas, when the weather cooperates." Dan began to sketch what he meant.

Emily stopped chopping red cabbage long enough to look over his shoulder. "I think the tables would look better around the outside of the converted barn."

"Doing it that way would offer a lot more natural shade," Dan agreed. Inspired, he began to draw a rough approximation of what they were talking about. "You could also configure it to put a small self-serve café in the retail space like they do in a lot of bookstores now. Either at the very center of the space or off to one side in the front. It wouldn't be as formal as a tearoom, but it would probably be more customer-friendly."

Emily went back to the counter and chopped up two Granny Smith apples and slid the pieces into the pan, along with the cabbage and thin slices of red onion. She wiped her hands on a towel and crossed to look over his shoulder again. "Actually," she said, smiling for the first time since they'd entered the kitchen, "I think I like that idea a lot."

Finally, Dan thought, they were on their way to a plan.

The only thing left to do was sell their ideas to Tex.

Dan used a software program on his laptop to create a three-dimensional vision of what he and Emily had talked about. He e-mailed it to Tex. And at eight-thirty that evening, the three of them connected via phone and Internet for a conference call.

"I like the idea of easing into the restaurant aspect of the business," Tex said. "But what about the house?"

"I'd like to live there with my baby," Emily said.

There was a silence on the other end of the connection.

"Are you sure you want to be that close to the retail space?" Tex asked at last. "During peach season, it will open at seven in the morning and close around nine at night. That's a long time to have people traipsing on and off the property, especially when you've got a little baby around. Instead, you both could, as we discussed, live in my parents' old home—rent free—as property manager."

Once again, Dan wondered if Tex was making a play for Emily.

"I'm going to want someone living in the house," Tex continued matter-of-factly. "Someone I can trust."

"You're still going to need somewhere to stay when you return to the property from time to time," Emily countered.

"I can stay in your parents' old place," Tex said. "The commerce won't bother me. And I'd appreciate being close to the construction as it unfolds." He paused. "I'm just thinking about what's best for you and the baby," he said.

Dan had to admit that what Tex was saying made sense.

Emily looked around, her fondness for the house they were sitting in evident. "I don't know, Tex," she murmured. "I'll have to think about it and get back to you."

And that, it seemed, was that.

Tex e-mailed Dan the budget his firm had for the plans to be drawn up, and also a firm schedule, as well as the limit for construction costs. Dan promised to get him something by the middle of the following week. They ended the call.

Looking a lot more relaxed, albeit still somewhat restless, Emily went to the fridge. She opened both compartments then shut them again.

"I can't believe it," she murmured.

Aware he had no valid reason to linger, Dan began packing up his computer. "What?"

Emily swung back to face him. She put a hand to her tummy, clearly distressed. "I'm hungry again!"

Dan strapped his computer between the protective pads in the carrying case. "I can't believe it, either," he said, chuckling affectionately. "We both ate like field hands." He tossed her an appreciative glance, thanking her for the effort. "Dinner was delicious, by the way."

Emily wrinkled her nose. Clearly unsatisfied, she complained, "It would have been better if we could have topped it off with German chocolate cake."

Dan saw no reason Emily couldn't have what she wanted most, now or at any other time. He set his briefcase aside, glad for a reason to delay. "I'm sure there are places in town we could still get a slice."

She studied him skeptically. "You'd really do that?"

And so much more—if you'd let me. But, wary of moving too fast, Dan put aside what he wanted—an entire night in her bed—and shrugged. "We've already done as much as we can or probably should today. Walt and the kids aren't expecting me back until tomorrow afternoon. It's Saturday night. We worked hard. Accomplished a lot, too. And—" he moved past her to peer out the window at the darkness of the November night "—it's stopped raining."

Emily glanced out the window, too. "You're right." She smiled. "It has."

"So what do you say?" Dan swung around to face her and took her hand in his. "Is it a date or not?"

ONCE AGAIN, EMILY THOUGHT, Dan had thrown her completely off her guard by making a move on her when she least expected it.

She swallowed around the sudden parched feeling in her throat. "Dan…"

He tugged her nearer, entwining their fingers as intimately as they had their bodies, earlier in the day.

Emily looked down at their clasped hands.

Dan continued softly, "We've made love twice. Had coffee together once. Yet never so much as shared a piece of cake."

He spoke as if it were a terrible tragedy.

And in a way, Emily thought, it was.

If only they were at the same point in their lives, or even planning to be in the same city after December first. Instead, she was starting a family; he was looking forward to a reprieve from the constant parental duties. She was likely moving home to Fredericksburg; Dan was remaining in Fort Worth, some four hours away. Once she became a lot more pregnant, travel that far would not be advisable.

And that left them nowhere.

Emily forced herself to be practical. With a smile, she offered gently, "Which is perhaps why we shouldn't go down that road."

Dan shrugged, not about to give up. "If we aren't going to be lovers—" he looked into her eyes "—can't we at least be friends?"

Chapter Nine

"Ohhhh," Emily moaned, not sure whether she was still in gastronomic heaven or about to be in overeating hell. Placing a hand to her sternum, she leaned against the outside wall of the German pastry shop on Fredericksburg's main drag. Inside, customers filled the tables, enjoying desserts every bit as decadent and luscious as the one she and Dan had just shared.

Discomfort radiated through the upper part of her chest. Stifling another moan of dismay, she gazed up at Dan, who was studying her with a mixture of amused indulgence and concern.

"I knew this was a mistake," Emily lamented as the first telltale wave of heartburn hit.

And so had Dan when he'd seen the size and richness of the combination German chocolate cheesecake covered in dark chocolate ganache and nuts and slathered with whipped cream. Considering the heavy dinner they'd just consumed, he'd wondered if perhaps the two of them shouldn't opt for something lighter. But Emily, her pregnancy-fueled appetite roaring, had insisted she had room for it all.

Now, of course, she wasn't so sure she had. Who said it was a good idea to give in to prenatal cravings? she wondered irritably.

Dan shook his head. Hand cupping her elbow, he steered her into the pharmacy next door.

"That may be the case," Dan observed drolly, "but it didn't stop you from eating the last bite of cake."

Okay, so for a few minutes there she'd been as out of control in the bakery café as she'd been in bed with him.

Wondering how she'd become such a hedonist, Emily narrowed her eyes at him. "Are you making fun of me?"

Dan slapped a hand to the center of his broad chest and regarded her with comically exaggerated innocence. "Me? No, ma'am. No way. No how."

More out of control emotionally than ever, Emily stamped her foot in a show of temper designed to distract her from the real issue—her inability to stop wanting more with him. More time, more lovemaking, more everything. "You're laughing!" she accused, indignant.

Dan's rich chuckle was music to her ears. "Can't help it," he confessed with an unrepentant grin. He tapped the tip of her nose. "You're very cute when you're pregnant."

Emily scoffed. "You've never seen me *not* pregnant, Dan."

Crinkles formed around his eyes. "True." His hand slid protectively around her as they moved closer to let another customer pass in the pharmacy aisle. "But I can imagine it."

That was the problem, Emily thought with a wistful sigh. She could imagine being with Dan for a lot longer than the next two weeks, too. Coming into town with him tonight had just made the fantasy all the more real. Warning herself not to get too carried away, she concentrated on the task at hand—getting something to quell her heartburn. "I have to stop eating so much," she said, shaking her head in remonstration.

"You still look very slender for someone who's nearly five months along," Dan soothed as they roamed the store looking for the liquid antacid Emily's doctor had said it was safe to take. His palm slid lower on her back. "Depending on what you wear," he added.

Emily shot him a glance. "I just look fat?"

Exasperation turned the corners of his mouth down. "That was *not* what I was going to say," he returned sternly.

Emily curved her palm over her baby bump and leaned back against the shelf, looking up at him. "Then what were you going to say?"

Dan braced a hand on the shelf, next to her head, and leaned down to whisper in her ear, "That you look cute all the time to me." He smiled.

A thrill shot through her.

Overwhelmed by her deepening emotions, she looked for the clouds in the silver lining. The problem that would keep her from falling head over heels in love with the sexy father of three.

"Not beautiful," Emily assumed, feeling another surge of wholly irrational pregnancy hormones soar through her again. "Just cute."

Looking ready to risk anything to be with her again, Dan curled a finger around a lock of her hair. "Why do I feel this is a trick question?" he asked, his gaze roving her upturned face.

Not sure where this was going—not sure where she wanted it to go—Emily wet her lips. "Just answer me," she prodded quietly.

Dan let his gaze slowly search her face. "I don't think you want me to do that," he said.

Emily swallowed around the sudden parched feeling in her throat. "Why not?"

"Because—" Dan sighed, looking as conflicted as she felt "—if I start telling you how incredibly beautiful I think you are every hour of every day, it's only going to lead to something we have both sworn off."

Emily released a long, slow breath. "We did that, didn't we?"

Dan held her eyes. "We agreed we would try just being friends for a while."

Another dumb idea, Emily thought. How often did she have romance and passion in her life? Not to mention the completely unforgettable kind Dan was offering? And yet here she was, throwing even a short-term fling away, all in the name of protecting her heart, which was getting broken anyway.

"Now what are you thinking?" Dan asked.

Emily pressed a fist against the increasing pressure in the center of her chest. Pressure she was no longer sure was all due to too much rich food. "That heartburn in a pregnant woman is no laughing matter."

He didn't buy it.

But it didn't matter, because as they proceeded a little farther down the aisle, they located what they were looking for. One transaction at the cash register later, they were outside again. Overhead the moon was clearly visible, and stars shone in the black velvet sky. The rain-scented breeze ruffled their hair.

Shivering a little, Emily uncapped the bottle and swigged the recommended dose of two tablespoons. The chalky liquid coated the inside of her mouth and slid down her throat. She made a face. "I know what the bottle says, but this is definitely not wild berry." She shuddered and made another face.

Dan watched, waited. "But it's helping," he said finally.

Emily leaned against the rough brick facade, liking the warmth of his body. "A lot." She made another face. "Now, if only I could do something about the yucky taste in my mouth." Before it brought on another bout of dreaded "morning sickness."

Dan reached into his pocket and pulled out a small roll of spearmint breath mints. "Maybe this will help."

Their fingers touched as the transfer was made.

Emily put a mint on her tongue. It did help.

"Better?" he asked.

Yes, Emily thought, in that the bad taste was gone. And no, in that her longing for him had just increased a hundredfold.

MONDAY AFTERNOON, DAN met Travis, Jack, Nate and Grady at a local grocery-store warehouse. They were all participating in the local food drive sponsored by the Fort Worth Community Service League. Travis was lending a truck from his construction company. The rest of them were loading up donated goods, which would be delivered to various shelters and food banks in the area.

It was more than a chance for Dan and his friends to get together, it was an opportunity for them to give back to the community that had given so much to them.

And today, Dan thought, it was also an opportunity for him to hit his pals up for a little help in another venue.

While they loaded cases of canned sweet potatoes and

green beans, Dan told his friends about his trip to Fredericksburg and enlisted their help in making Emily's dreams come true.

"I'll ask around, see who's the best in the area for that type of construction," Travis said.

"Same here with the wiring, computer and communication systems," Jack promised.

Nate pushed a dolly loaded with boxes onto the truck bed. "I'll spread the word to all my clients, see if anyone is interested in buying bulk produce from them or underwriting the construction of a restaurant and tearoom," Nate added.

The latter of which, Dan planned to surprise Emily with. "Thanks," he said.

Grady went back into the warehouse for a load of frozen turkeys. When he returned he asked, "How are things going otherwise? Mealtime any better?"

"Lots, actually," Dan said, thinking about what a change Emily had made to his home life.

"Do you worry about the kids getting too attached to her?" Jack pushed the empty dolly down the truck bed. "Thinking of her as a mother figure or anything?"

It wasn't just the kids, Dan thought. He could easily envision Emily as the woman of his house. And that was a dangerous notion. "They know she's planning on leaving us right after the Thanksgiving holiday weekend to move to Fredericksburg."

Nate studied Jack. The most analytical of the group and the only one who didn't have kids, he was always considering every angle of a situation. "You haven't tried to convince her to stay on? Work for your family permanently?"

"No," Dan said.

"Why not, if it's working out so well?" Travis loaded boxes of baby formula and cereal.

Grady grinned like the newlywed he was. "I think I know. Having Emily work for his family complicates things in a way that puts a wrench in other things...."

Leave it to Grady to figure it out, Dan mused.

Not ready to discuss feelings that were still way too raw and unexpected, Dan turned the discussion to another aspect of the situation that was a heck of a lot easier to talk about. "She made it clear to me from the very beginning that she wants to turn things around for the orchard her father started."

The guys considered that. Dan had an idea what they were thinking: there he went again, giving his heart to another woman on a crusade that would end up leaving him in her rearview mirror.

Grady stacked boxes of smoked hams near the door of the truck. Because they had to be refrigerated, they would be last on and first off. "Couldn't she let the guy she's going into business with do that?"

If only they'd just been talking about growing fruit here! It would be a lot easier for Emily to walk away and move on with her life.

Dan vetoed the suggested possibility with a shake of his head. "Tex Ostrander doesn't have the culinary expertise to start a restaurant or develop products to sell in the retail space. Emily does." It was an incredible business opportunity for her, the start of a whole new career that still had the connection to her past she craved. Dan couldn't compete with that, no matter how much he wanted to.

Travis closed the back of the supply truck and secured

the latch. "It sounds like a real opportunity for Emily, but what about you? How do you feel? You want her working closely with that guy?"

Dan hadn't told anyone what was going on with him and Emily. But his friends had seen him when he first laid eyes on her, and knew him well enough to recognize the chemistry brewing between them.

"Yeah, you said he was her ex-fiancé," Grady remarked.

They all waited to see Dan's reaction.

Dan shrugged and tugged off his work gloves. "Why should I care?"

Glances were exchanged all around.

"Not the same as answering the question," Nate teased.

Jack grinned devilishly. "Maybe he's into her."

Travis, the most cynical of the group, said, "Be careful, buddy. We were around to help you pick up the pieces the last time a woman left you to fulfill her dreams." He clamped a hand on Jack's shoulder. "We don't want to have to do it again."

"Do you think Mommy is going to like my pilgrim?" Kayla asked as she put her latest school art project on the bulletin board in the kitchen.

Emily smiled. "I think she's going to love it."

Kayla beamed.

Tommy came in the back door, bag of athletic gear over his shoulder. "Hey, Em? Do you think you can teach me how to make a fruit smoothie? The coach said they're good for hydrating us."

And, Emily thought, they supplied vital nutrients, too. "Sure thing." She went to the well-stocked fridge. "You want one with your dinner?"

"Can I have one, too?" Ava asked, looking up from her thick textbook. "I haven't had enough fruit today, either."

Emily got out the blender and set it on the counter. "Coming right up."

Ten minutes and one culinary lesson later, they were all sipping fruit smoothies. "You're really good at that," Tommy said.

Ava nodded. "You ought to teach kids how to cook."

Kayla smiled through a smoothie mustache. "I'd come!"

Happiness bubbled through Emily. And suddenly she felt it—the kick of a tiny foot or fist against the inside of her abdomen.

As always when it happened, she went very still, not wanting to miss a moment of her baby's attempt to communicate with her.

Ava's glance slid to her tummy and the hand Emily had unconsciously shifted there. "Is the baby kicking?"

Emily nodded as another, harder kick hit her just above the waist.

"Can I feel it?" Kayla asked in excitement.

Emily grinned. "Sure." She held Kayla's hand against her tummy, hoping the baby would cooperate. The baby did.

Kayla's eyes widened. "Wow!" she said. "Feel it, Ava!"

Looking both thrilled and apprehensive, Ava edged nearer.

For a moment Emily feared the baby would not cooperate, but he or she eventually did. Then it was Tommy's turn. And the baby showed off with the biggest wallop to the wall of Emily's abdomen yet.

All three kids grinned. "That was somethin'," Tommy said.

"He's really rowdy!" Kayla agreed.

"It might be a *she*," Ava countered. "But you're right. The baby is really moving around in there!"

And that was when Emily looked up and saw Dan standing there. She had no idea how long he'd been observing them. Clearly long enough to realize all three of his kids had felt her baby kick.

Kayla rushed over to him and wrapped her arms around his middle. "Daddy, did we kick like that when we were in Mommy's tummy?"

Dan tore his gaze from Emily's and looked down at his daughter. "Absolutely. In fact, you guys were all so rowdy I thought you were practicing to be rodeo cowboys."

Kayla giggled. The older two rolled their eyes at their dad's joke.

Walt came in and went straight to the sink to wash up. "Dinner ready? I'm starving!"

"Just about," Emily said.

Ava moved to the computer on the kitchen desk. "Look!" she said. "It's an e-mail from Mom!"

DAN HADN'T THOUGHT IT WAS possible to be that disappointed. Again.

His kids still reeling, he passed on the opportunity to defend their mom and went straight to his study. Picked up the phone. And punched in the emergency number, routed through the International Children's Medical Service.

As soon as he got her voice mail, he said tersely, "Brenda, you can't keep doing this to the kids. Either come home when you promise or stay away altogether!"

Furious, he slammed the phone down and looked up, to see Emily standing in the doorway.

She shut the study door behind her.

Disapproval glittered in her eyes. Her voice and demeanor carried a wealth of worry. "Kayla's crying—she ran off to her room. Ava went up to comfort her. Tommy stomped outside. He and Walt are talking by the woodpile."

Dan exhaled.

Figuring there was more, he waited. It wasn't long in coming.

"You should have stayed and comforted them."

"I'm too furious myself to be of any use. Besides, there's nothing to say."

Emily regarded him with a crusader's zeal. "How about 'I'm sorry—I know you are all disappointed and I wish things were different'?"

Dan ignored the knot in his gut—the same one he felt whenever his ex was careless with his kids' feelings. "They know that."

Emily gave him a chiding look. "Do they?"

The room reverberated with an angry silence. Dan stalked to the window. One of his neighbors was decorating for the holidays, placing a giant horn of plenty on their front door. Thanksgiving was almost upon them. And once again, thanks to the carelessness of his ex, his kids were going to feel neglected by their mom. Worse, he knew they would take it personally—not just now, but likely for the rest of their lives. His being hurt was one thing—he'd long gotten past the disappointment of his failed marriage. His kids being hurt was something else entirely.

Dan gritted his teeth. "I am so tired of her doing this to them."

"I'll bet."

"You don't understand."

"I think I do."

And she still thought he was wrong.

Frustration bubbled up inside him. "My kids need a mother."

She perched on the edge of his desk, arms folded in front of her, obviously prepared to listen.

Dan swallowed. Needing her to understand, he forged on, "One of the reasons they've had such a hard time this past year is that there's no steady female presence in their lives."

Emily's expression gave away nothing. "Which is where I come in."

Dan could tell by her tone he had made her feel more a means to an end than a dream come true for all of them. He worked to make amends. "You've seen how they respond to you."

She tensed, seemingly on guard once more. No doubt she was as loath to the idea of being hurt as he was. "They like me as a family friend, Dan."

Is that all she wants to be? Dan looked deep into her eyes. "I think it's more than that."

Another beat of silence fell between them. "We're getting off the subject," Emily said.

Dan lifted a silencing palm. "I don't want to talk about Brenda. Or the situation," he returned gruffly. "It would just be a waste of time."

Emily's eyes filled with compassion. "Dan..." She reached out to him, in an apparent bid to make him calm down, listen to her...accept her help.

And all he really wanted was to take her up on her offer of comfort, haul her into his arms, forget the hardships of divorce and lose himself in the moment. It would have happened, too, had he not had a houseful of kids and a boatload of parental responsibilities demanding his attention. Upstairs, he heard the clatter of feet and the muffled sounds of both girls sobbing their hearts out.

Barely containing his own emotions, Dan strode past Emily. "I'll get them down to dinner as soon as I can. Given the situation," he growled, "it may take a while."

EMILY WAITED UNTIL DAN LEFT.

Her own feelings in turmoil, she remained there, trying to calm down. Then, knowing what she had to do, she shut the door to the study, closing herself inside, and went over to Dan's desk.

There, front and center, was his address book, open to the page with the phone number for emergency contact.

She picked up the phone and began to dial.

She got patched through to Brenda's voice mail, just as Dan had.

Her message to his ex was a lot different from what his had been.

Finished, she put the phone back down.

This was either going to help or make things a whole heck of a lot worse, she realized shakily. She could only hope it was the former.

Chapter Ten

Early the next morning Emily was just walking out the front door of her building, bag slung over her shoulder and pushcart in hand, when she saw Dan walking toward her. Sunglasses only partially concealing the grim expression on his face, he caught up with her on the sidewalk.

"We need to talk," he said.

She'd been afraid of that. Reminding herself that she had done the right thing—even if it wasn't what Dan wanted or expected—Emily gestured in the direction she intended to go. "I'm on the way to the farmers' market on North Henderson." Which luckily was within a few blocks of her loft. "One of my regular clients needs me to prepare a luncheon for her bridge club."

"I'll come with you."

Emily picked up her pace and Dan matched her stride. "I got a very interesting e-mail this morning," he began.

Emily swore silently. She had been hoping Brenda would do what she suggested when they talked. Obviously Dan's ex had not. "Really?" Finding the temperature a little warmer than she'd expected, Emily used her free hand to unfasten the first two buttons on her wool jacket.

Anger flashed in his eyes. "It had Brenda's flight information on it."

Her heartbeat accelerating, Emily stopped at the corner and waited for the light to change. "That's good, isn't it?" Deliberately she ignored the mixture of disappointment and fatigue on his face.

His expression did not change.

"Walt and the kids got the same e-mail."

A large man tried to squeeze in beside her at the crosswalk. Emily edged closer to Dan, taking in the soap and fresh-air scent clinging to his skin. "So?"

The light changed before Dan could answer her. Emily guided the wheels of her personal-shopping tote over the lip of the curb and onto the street. As she did so, one of the wheels got stuck in a crack in the asphalt.

Before she could even attempt to free it, Dan reached over and plucked the stainless-steel carryall from her grasp and switched it to his other hand. He slid a protective hand beneath her elbow and proceeded to escort her across the street before the light could change again. "So Brenda has apparently changed her mind again," Dan said gruffly. "Now she *is* coming for Thanksgiving."

Emily tried not to look too relieved. She hadn't known how her meddling would work out. She swallowed and turned her gaze to Dan as they proceeded past the crush of morning traffic crowding the city streets. "I'm sure the kids will be happy about that."

"I'm sure they will be—if it happens. If she isn't jerking them around again."

Wishing she could take Dan in her arms and comfort him physically without it leading to anything, Emily reassured softly, "I don't think she is going to do that."

"Really."

"Really." Her voice was as firm as his was skeptical.

They paused at another crosswalk. Silence fell.

The light changed.

They pushed through the last intersection before the market and into the throng of avid shoppers. One of the first booths contained a display of fresh-baked goods. The aroma of sweet rolls and coffee was incredibly tempting. Catching the look of longing on her face, Dan stopped in front of the display. "What would you like?"

Emily forced herself to be practical. "Maybe on the way out." She needed her hands for shopping.

Dan told the clerk, "I'll have a large coffee—black."

He paid and they continued on with Dan wordlessly simmering at her side.

The pressure became too much. Emily didn't want any tension between them, and she really didn't want any secrets.

"Fine," she said. She swung around to face him, prepared to go toe-to-toe, if need be. "I called Brenda."

That he'd apparently already deduced on his own. His eyes narrowed. "How'd you get the number?"

Emily raised her shoulders in halfhearted defense. "From your desk."

At his glare, Emily propped her hands on her hips. "Well, someone had to do it!"

Storm clouds gathered in his eyes. "Now you sound like Walt."

Emily got back to the business of shopping. "Walt's right, in this instance." She paused in front of the fishmonger. She studied the day's catch, then placed an order for six pounds of fresh salmon.

While it was being wrapped up, she turned back to Dan. "I heard your message to Brenda. It wasn't exactly friendly."

Dan fumed while Emily paid. "I had every right to be angry with Brenda." He pushed the cart to the next venue, a vegetable stand.

Emily gathered bunches of fresh asparagus and field greens, along with lemons and dill. "I am sure you know that sugar works better than vinegar every time."

"Is that what you did? Sweet-talked her?" Dan demanded.

Emily felt herself flush. "Brenda called me back last night and we talked. I told her how much the kids miss her. How much they'd been looking forward to her visit and how devastated they were that she'd gone back to her original plan and wouldn't be back in the States again until Christmas."

"And?" His tone was brusque.

Emily took a deep breath and replied, "Brenda was torn. She wants to be here for both holidays, but she can't be. She doesn't have that much time off. But she wants to spend all the vacation time she does have with her kids."

Dan was silent. The anger went out of him at last.

Emily explained the solution she had offered Brenda. "I suggested that you could put up the tree the day after Thanksgiving and the kids could have their own Christmas celebration a month early with Brenda. I even offered to supply the dinner for them. That way the kids can have two Christmases. One with you, and one with her."

Dan pushed the cart to the next venue. "What did she say?"

Emily looked at Dan, unable to hide the traitorous emotion rising up within her. "Brenda wants Christmas with her kids." Emily paused, unable to help the catch in her voice. "She said it had been too long. That she misses them, too."

IT WAS OFFICIAL, DAN THOUGHT, as he watched Emily. He felt like the world's biggest jerk. "So Brenda really is coming?" he said again for his kids' sake, almost afraid to hope.

Emily walked toward the florist on the next aisle over. Her posture as self-confident as her voice, she looked at Dan and confirmed, "Brenda really is coming for the entire Thanksgiving week. But this time, she wants to grab a cab and go straight to her hotel when she arrives."

Another problem loomed. Dan frowned. "Walt and the kids usually pick her up."

"I know." Emily's voice was sympathetic. "Brenda told me. But she's got a twenty-six-hour journey that crosses multiple time zones. She probably won't have slept and definitely won't have showered. She said, in the past it's been a problem because the kids take her travel-dazed state personally—they think she's not glad to see them and she is. Anyway, the plan is, she'll get cleaned up and nap and then call Walt and the kids. And they can pick her up at the hotel."

Dan hesitated. "Walt will probably be okay with that. He's as independent in his own way as Brenda is in hers, but I'm not sure the kids will understand her wanting to do it this way."

Emily stepped nearer. Her eyes were full of the strength and compassion every parent needed. "It's up to you to make them understand, Dan," she told him, as fierce as any mama bear protecting her cubs. She moved even closer, the scent of her hair and skin inundating his senses. "Ava and Tommy are old enough to get what it is to be so physically exhausted you can barely stay on your feet, never mind make coherent conversation. And while Kayla might not be old enough, she can certainly understand that her mommy doesn't want to feel all 'travel-icky' when they see each other. That her mommy wants a chance to take a bath and put on clean clothes first."

Emily released a beleaguered sigh and stepped back again. "Not that the kids could have gone to the airport to greet her this time. If you took a good look at her flight itinerary, you'll see that Brenda's flying in Monday morning—the kids will all be in school."

Dan exhaled thoughtfully. "Which makes them going a moot point."

"Right." Emily paused long enough to inhale the fragrance of the flowers in her arms. "Anyway, I told her I'd make a dinner in advance and leave it in the fridge so she and Walt and the kids could have their privacy."

Dan caught her arm and held it gently. "Thanks for calling her."

Emily leaned into his touch for a moment, before extricating herself and gracefully stepping away. She dipped her head in a nod, then handed money to the cashier, collected her change and moved on once again. "Consider it my gift to you, too."

She bent to settle the flowers among the other packages in her cart. Then, finished shopping, she turned her cart toward the exit.

Once again Dan fell into step beside her and took over pushing the cart. "I owe you."

Emily shook her head. "No, you don't. This was something I wanted to do. It kind of makes up for—" Abruptly her voice caught and she was unable to go on.

Catching the telltale glint of moisture in her eyes, Dan wrapped his arm about her waist. He knew she was emotional these days, but this seemed deeper than mere pregnancy hormones. "What?" he asked gently as they stepped off to the side.

Emily shook her head as if the action would help ward off the tears. "It kind of makes up for the years I spent estranged from my own mother," she finished in a low, rusty-sounding voice. "Your kids need Brenda in their lives, Dan. Whenever, however, they can get her."

Dan shrugged, his long-held resentment resurfacing. "Which is exactly why Brenda shouldn't have left them in the first place."

Suddenly furious, Emily threw up her arms in exasperation. "Coulda, woulda, shoulda! We all have stuff in our lives we wish was different, Dan. Stuff that should have happened and didn't. And we can spend our lives lamenting those things, or just deal with what is. I choose to do the latter." She shot him a withering gaze. "Your kids are never going to be happy unless they stop resenting the choices your ex-wife made and start embracing them. It sounds like Brenda's doing tremendous things for children all over the world—children who are in trouble, who have medical needs that aren't being met. You should be tremendously proud of that. So should your kids."

Her words were right on target and they stung.

Emily beseeched him with a tender touch. "Look, I know the kids feel deserted by Brenda. I see that." Her lower lip quivered. "I feel their pain. And I can only imagine how hard it is for you, as their father, to stand by helplessly as they've been hurt not just once but over and over again." She let out a long, tremulous breath. "But you can't change any of that, and you're going to have to find a way to make peace with the choices Brenda has made if you want your children to accept them, too."

DAN SPENT THE REST OF THE DAY thinking about what Emily had said to him. She had braved his wrath to do what was in the best interest of his kids, helped him come around to a more objective way of thinking about this situation. Whether she realized it or not, he owed her for that...and so much more. In an effort to demonstrate his gratitude, he left work early, stopped by the florist and headed home, in advance of both Walt and the kids.

To his disappointment, Emily wasn't there when he arrived. When another hour had passed, the girls and Walt were all home and there was still no word from her, he tried to reach her on her cell and then at home. There was no answer at either number.

When another hour passed, and he still hadn't heard from her, he began to get worried. So he drove over to her place and rang the bell. Once. Twice. Finally, on the third try, the lock clicked.

Emily opened the door. She was wearing an autumn-yellow chef's smock and tan cords. Brightly colored wool socks adorned her feet. Her hair was tousled and her eyes sleepy. She yawned and blinked hard, as if trying to make sense of what he was doing there. Never mind with a vase of pink lilies in one hand.

"What's going on?" she asked, smothering another yawn with the back of her hand.

Dan leaned against the doorjamb, thinking how beautiful she was at this very moment and how he would give anything to find a way to keep her in his life. Not just for his children's sake, but for his own. Because she was, undoubtedly, the best thing that had ever happened to him.

He smiled. "I was about to ask you the same question. You didn't show up for work."

Emily glanced at her watch, then at the darkening sky outside the windows. "Omigosh!"

Dan cupped a hand over her shoulder, stopping her before she could rush off in a tizzy. "Relax. Tommy has a wrestling meet this evening—it doesn't start until seven and he's having dinner with the team. Walt is taking the girls out for pizza."

"I can't believe I fell asleep!" Emily ushered Dan in and switched on lights as she went. "I only meant to lie down for a second." She shoved her hands through her hair, still looking a little disoriented. She focused on the vase. "And you brought me flowers?"

Her stunned, slightly bemused expression made him think he should have chosen something a little less romantic than pink lilies. "I wanted to say thank-you for talking to Brenda and getting her to change her mind about coming home for Thanksgiving."

"Oh." Emily's expression went flat. "No problem," she murmured. "I was happy to help." She carried the vase to the breakfast bar and set it down.

Dan followed. "So." He cleared his throat. "How'd your luncheon go?"

"Great. I got several more requests for holiday gigs from some of the guests in attendance. Another couple on my machine. I guess word is beginning to spread that I haven't left Fort Worth yet."

And if he was very lucky, Dan thought, she might decide to stay a good while longer. Long enough for the two of them to make what had started out as an impulsive fling turn into something more serious and longer lasting.

He paused deliberately, then met her eyes. "Are you going to take the gigs?" As expected, his question made her tense.

Emily bit into her lower lip. "I haven't quite decided."

Just as she hadn't quite decided if she was going to go into partnership with Tex Ostrander, Dan thought, comforted to realize that Emily was still contemplating all her options.

He could only hope that when the time came, she would make the decision that would pave the way for them to be together, instead of ensure they would not be.

In the meantime, they had this rare moment without kids, work or distraction of any kind. Dan looked around curiously. Filled moving boxes were stacked everywhere.

Emily strode over to the living-room area of the loft.

Dan watched, taking in her soft curves, and knew if he didn't keep the conversation going, they'd end up doing something completely insensible again.

Emily scooped a stack of brochures off the sofa, where, apparently, she'd been sleeping. "I try and pack a little every chance I get." She piled the velour throw and pillow in the center and sat down on one end. "Have a seat." She gestured to the other.

Dan settled opposite her, aware the linens formed a barrier every bit as effective as an old-fashioned bundling bed.

Acknowledging that wasn't such a bad move on her part—given that he'd like nothing more than to haul her onto his lap and kiss her right now—he looked at the papers spread across the coffee table instead.

Friends. They were trying to be just friends....

"What's all this?" he asked.

Emily tucked her legs beneath her and sat, cross-legged, against the arm of the sofa. She grabbed the pillow and held it to her chest, snug against her breasts. "It's information from the hospital in Fredericksburg. I have to register there for the birth if I plan to have the baby there. And select a doctor." Emily inhaled, looking overwhelmed. "Currently there are seven doctors delivering babies at the women's pavilion there. And my obstetrician here wants me to pick one before I move. We're supposed to talk about it when I go in to have my ultrasound the day after Thanksgiving. I've looked at all their profiles and talked to two so far on the phone."

Dan leaned toward her. "And?"

"They were nice…but I really like Dr. Markham, my doctor here. She saw me through the whole getting-pregnant process."

He watched Emily run her fingers through her hair, absently restoring order to the silky, sleep-mussed strands. "So you don't want to switch?"

Emily shook her head. "It's silly, I know."

"You could have the baby here," Dan suggested. "Move to Fredericksburg after you delivered, when things are more settled."

For a moment she looked tempted. Dan's hopes rose. Then she sighed and shook her head. "I really need to be at the farm to oversee the construction of the orchard's retail store. Speaking of which…"

Dan knew where this was going. Tex had e-mailed him something earlier in the day, and copied her on it. "I'm looking for local subcontractors now. I should have a written bid ready to present to you and Tex by the end of the week."

Emily smiled. "Great."

Dan slipped back into business mode. "Want to set something up for Friday at my office?"

"Absolutely. Just call and let me know what time."

"Will do."

She unfolded her legs and rose. "I'm going to have a glass of milk. Would you like some?"

Dan threw caution to the wind. "Actually—" he stood, too "—I'd like to take you to dinner."

Her elegant brows rose in surprise.

Aware he might be pushing too hard, too fast, Dan backed off with an excuse he knew she could readily accept. "It'll have to be short. I promised Tommy I'd be at the high-school gym to see his match. But it would give us a chance to discuss some of the finer points of the retail store. It'll make a big difference in the preliminary bid."

Emily relaxed. "I'll be ready to go in ten minutes," she said.

THIS WASN'T A DATE, Emily kept telling herself as she put on a sophisticated black maternity dress and ran a brush through her hair.

But it felt like a date.

Just as practically every moment alone with Dan did.

She really had to get a grip.

Unless Tex insisted they go with another firm—something she would fight—Dan was going to be the architect on this project. She would be in touch with him constantly…for business.

She would no longer be living in Fort Worth or cooking for his family or seeing him nearly every day. The intimacy of their contact would lessen drastically.

It wasn't like she was going to be in shape for anything more for too much longer, anyway, Emily reminded herself sternly. Her tummy was expanding, and although Dan didn't seem to mind making love to her, she knew as her pregnancy progressed, that might not still be the case.

She needed to be grateful for what passion they had shared.

The only problem was, she wanted to make love to him again.

She always wanted to make love to him, she realized wistfully. Wanted to be in love with him and have him love her back. And something in her told her that would never change. No matter where she lived or how much time passed…or how big her waistline got. Or what different timelines they were on, when it came to having a family…

Fortunately for Emily's fragile state of mind, time constraints necessitated that the two of them get down to business as soon as they were seated.

During the appetizers, they discussed the cost of various building materials. They were briefly interrupted when Emily was approached by a former client who wanted her to do a Thanksgiving-week brunch. Emily had enjoyed working for the woman before so she said yes and promised to call her later to discuss it.

During the salad course, Dan asked Emily just how rustic the inside of the retail store should be, and they discussed the various ways they could accomplish that. Between bites of the main course, they talked about where the elevators should be located. They had to put their strategy session on hold again when Emily was spotted by yet another former client, this one wanting her to do a luncheon. Emily knew the job would pay handsomely and would be creatively satisfying so she said yes.

"Sorry about that," Emily said when the businesswoman finally left the table.

Dan shrugged as he took a sip of water. A businessman himself, he understood. "It's a busy time of year for everyone in the food business."

Still… "I shouldn't have taken the luncheon gig earlier today, after already figuratively closing the doors on my business."

Dan leveled his gaze on hers. The sincerity in his eyes had her heart hammering in her chest. "But you wanted to do it."

Emily pleated the fabric of the starched linen tablecloth between her thumb and index finger. "What can I say?" She studied him right back. "The money's good." She was unable to suppress a rueful smile. "And there's probably a little ego involved, too."

Dan reached over to take her hand in his, stilling the restless motion of her fingers. "How so?"

She sat back against the sumptuous leather booth and he let go of her hand. "I worked hard to establish myself as one of the best personal chefs in Fort Worth." Knowing the best way to keep her relationship with Dan uncomplicated was to maintain a light tone, she continued with an offhand shrug and a self-effacing quirk of her lips. "I get so many compliments when I cook for someone. I know my food makes people happy." *It's made you and your family happy.* Emily swallowed around the tightness of her throat. "It's difficult to walk away from that." *Almost as difficult as it is to walk away from you.*

"Then why are you?" Dan asked. He held up a palm before she could respond. "I know you want to be part of the effort to revitalize the orchard your parents started. But there's nothing that says you have to move to Fredericksburg before the birth of your baby in April." He looked at her intently. "You could stay here. Continue cooking for my family, take extra gigs, maybe even hire some help to keep Chef for Hire going indefinitely while you oversee the building of the retail store and tearoom at the orchard."

Emily was unsure if he was asking for her convenience—or his. All she knew for certain was that it wasn't the kind of proposal she wanted from Dan. She rubbed her palm over the baby kicking inside her belly, every ounce of maternal protectiveness coming to the fore. "Are you forgetting I'm pregnant?"

His glance roamed her curvy shape.

Apparently not, Emily thought.

She swallowed once again and continued, "I'd have to be superhuman to do all that."

Dan sat back, too, his countenance indomitable. "Okay, then, forget the extra gigs. Just cook for my family while you get the orchard business up and running."

"Tex—"

"Simultaneously oversees several different businesses, in different parts of the state, too."

Okay, so it wasn't Tex she had the problem with right now, Emily acknowledged, working to keep her out-of-control emotions in check. "My deal with him requires I reside on the premises."

Dan tensed. "Have you signed anything yet?"

"No." Emily tried not to feel too relieved. "The partnership agreement is still being drawn up. It won't be official until after Thanksgiving."

"Then there's still time to negotiate." Dan leaned forward and took her hand in his again. "Get what you want out of this arrangement. Don't let Tex steamroll you, Emily. You're tougher and more astute than that."

It wasn't Tex that Emily was having trouble handling. The difficulty was with her growing feelings for Dan.

She looked down at their intertwined hands, amazed at how natural—how right—his protective grip felt. "You're forgetting another aspect of this problem," she forced herself to say. "I have to be out of my loft by the end of the month. I'm going to have to move somewhere."

Dan shrugged. "Fort Worth has plenty of available housing of all kinds."

Emily disengaged their hands. "None that would be rent-free—which is what Tex is offering."

"There's one place," Dan said, more determined than ever. "You could move in with me."

Chapter Eleven

Emily stared at Dan in shock. "Whoa there, fella!"

Okay, so his wasn't his most eloquent proposition ever, Dan admonished himself. But it was probably the most forthright. "It's not like I'm asking you to bunk in with me." *Or sleep with me.* Having the kids around would put an end to those thoughts, tempting as they were. "We have a guest room."

"That not even your ex-wife uses," Emily pointed out.

Dan concentrated on the presumptuous gleam in her eyes. "Only because Brenda prefers to stay in a hotel when she's in town. Otherwise, awkward as it might be, I would be happy to put her up for the kids' sake."

Her posture militant, Emily sat back in her chair and folded her arms. The action pushed up her breasts so their soft roundness spilled out of the sexy V-neck of her dress. A heart-shaped pendant nestled in the hollow of her alabaster skin. "And your offer to me is for the kids' sake, too. Because you want the kids to continue to have home-cooked meals."

"Of course," he said, though that wasn't the entire truth. Yes, she'd brought wonderful changes to his house. And all three of his children were happier than they'd been since their mother had left to take a job overseas. But for the first time in years he had a spring in his step and joy in his heart…

However, his glib offer was, and would remain, a strictly business proposition. Until such time that Emily's talents as a chef were no longer needed in his household, and then he would be free to pursue her the way he had wanted to pursue her from the very first.

Emily relaxed slightly.

Encouraged, Dan continued his sales pitch. "It's not that unorthodox an arrangement. Lots of people have personal chefs who live in."

Emily tensed.

Dan swore silently to himself. Clearly a wrong move where she was concerned. What was the matter with him? Once again, he forced himself to go on with strictly professional enthusiasm. "It could be for a few days or even weeks."

"I appreciate the offer." Emily offered a brisk smile. "But staying under your roof would feel too much like living with you, in the same way that working in your home, cooking dinner for your family almost every night, feels pretty intimate, too. As I told you, I got into trouble that way before—I don't want it to happen again."

Dan saw her swallow, saw the vulnerable light back in her eyes. She looked down and ran her fingertips over the condensation on her water glass, gently rubbing at the moisture until it disappeared. "It's one of the reasons I'm really looking forward to meeting Brenda when she comes in next week." Her throat sounded as if it were clogged with tears. "I need to remind myself that as much as the kids might need and want a mom in their lives, as much as they've turned to me that way in the last two weeks, they still have a mother." She gulped again, trembling this time. "And it's not me."

Emily moved her hand to the swell of her tummy. Rubbing the area lovingly, she said, "Happily, this time, I do have a child of my own. And as such, I have to do what's right for my baby—and that's create a whole new life that will allow me to be with my child every day and every night."

"So you're headed to Fredericksburg on December first?" Dan asked, unable to contain his disappointment.

"If the partnership agreement is signed by then, yes," Emily confirmed.

"THE THING IS," DAN TOLD his friends the next afternoon when they had finished their joint-work session at the McCabe Building in downtown Fort Worth, "I'd really appreciate it if you all would put out the word that Emily may not be closing Chef for Hire after all—at least not right away—and is taking on jobs for the holiday season. Through Thanksgiving, but I think she could be persuaded to do some Christmas and New Year's gigs, too."

Nate, Grady, Travis and Jack exchanged looks as the five of them gathered up the plans and notes spread across the large piece of plywood that had served as their conference table in the unfinished executive floor for Nate's company.

Grimacing at the sound of the nail gun being used in the framing of a set of rooms to their right, Grady asked, "Does she know you're doing this on her behalf?"

"No. And I'd rather she didn't." Dan rolled up the amended blueprints and slid them into the carrying case.

"Because?" Nate queried.

Dan strode to the tinted windows, overlooking the Trinity River. "She'd probably think I'm interfering."

"Aren't you?" Grady asked.

"Emily has doubts about what she's doing," Dan said, pushing away his guilt. "I think she would have called off her move to Fredericksburg if she didn't feel duty-bound to help restore the orchard her father started."

"Why is that your problem?" Travis asked, shutting down his laptop.

"Because I owe her—for everything she's done for me and my kids the past few weeks."

Another round of looks was exchanged. The recently married Grady slapped a companionable hand on Dan's shoulder. "We all know you swore off marriage when you got divorced."

"Maybe it's time you reconsidered," Jack said kindly.

Dan resented the advice. "I'm just trying to help her out because I don't want to see her make a mistake."

"The only mistake I see here is you not being honest with yourself," Nate interjected bluntly. "Face it, buddy. I'm the devoted bachelor—you're the marrying kind."

Dan swallowed as the unsolicited advice hit a little too close to home.

"Any idea whether she's having a boy or a girl?" Grady asked.

"No," Dan said, wondering where that had come from. He looked at his friends, beginning to get really irked now at all this interference regarding his love life. "What does that matter?"

Nate jumped in with, "Sons need fathers around."

"It'd be a point in your favor," Jack added helpfully.

"Should you ever decide to put aside your fear and go after Emily the way you obviously want to," Grady teased.

Grimacing, Dan realized the guys were right. He was

kidding himself, thinking he could let Emily go without first giving their relationship a real shot. The kind of connection they had came along once in a lifetime if you were lucky. He'd be a fool to ignore it.

"Speaking of beautiful women…" Nate murmured.

The service elevator had halted at the other end of the mostly open floor. Looking wonderful in a red chef's coat, jeans and yellow hard hat required by anyone prowling the half-constructed interior of the building, Emily stepped out of the metal cage. She had a bag slung over one shoulder and a folder in her hand. Seeing Dan, she lifted a hand.

"Good luck, buddy," Jack said.

His pals headed toward the elevator. Heart kicking against his ribs, Dan stayed right where he was. As Emily neared him, the sound of a jackhammer from the floor below reverberated.

Wincing at the earsplitting noise, only partially muffled by the solid wall of concrete between them, she cupped a hand around her mouth. "I was going to ask if you had a minute to talk to me!"

Dan knew it must be important if she'd sought him out here. The problem was, the noise level here was intrusive, no matter which of the thirty-nine floors they were on. And although the exterior of the sleek stone-and-glass building was completed, the inside floors were nothing but open shells.

Mindful of his schedule, he glanced at his watch, then steered her back toward the elevator. When the noise abated to the point he could speak without shouting to be heard, he said, "Sure. If you don't mind riding down to the first floor with me. In half an hour I'm meeting a client there who wants to put in a clothing store."

"It shouldn't take long," she said. "I want your opinion on these contracts."

Which meant, Dan thought, there was something she didn't like. And she wanted confirmation that she was right to feel concerned.

Still, inserting himself in her business carried with it a certain risk. Dan followed her into the cage and pressed the buttons. He stayed in the center of the steel-mesh-enclosed cage. "What does your lawyer say?"

Emily turned her glance from the exposed rails and gears of the lift. Looking as if she felt a little leery in the construction apparatus, she stepped toward the middle, a little closer to him. She braced herself as the elevator went down. "My lawyer said I'm lucky to be offered a partnership where I'm not expected to put up any cash at signing, that will allow me to live on the land rent- and utility-free as caretaker, and share equally in the profits."

The elevator stopped at one. Because Dan had a design consultation with the prospective owners, no building was currently going on. Grateful for the absence of construction noise, Dan stepped out onto the floor. He led the way down the long interior corridor to the back door of the proposed clothing shop. "And yet you have qualms."

Emily nodded. "Taking a job that offers fully paid health insurance and lodging but no guaranteed salary is a risk. I guess I didn't realize how much of one until I saw it all in writing."

Dan shut the door behind them. He watched Emily take off her yellow hard hat and set it down. "So," he said, as he did the same with his, "if you have a good peach crop…"

"And the retail and tearoom business takes off like Tex expects, then I'll be sitting pretty by the end of the year, in terms of my half of the profits. I'll have doubled or tripled what I could have made as a personal chef."

"But if you have a bad crop…" Dan opened the carrying case that held the preliminary plans for the clothing shop.

"Which we both know could happen, given the highly unpredictable weather in the spring." Her expression pensive, Emily watched him spread out the plans on the table that had been set up in the center of the space. "Then I'd have run through all the money I saved for the down payment on the orchard. And the retail business depends on us getting prime fruit to attract customers in the first place."

Dan set up his laptop computer, too. "What was the plan to compensate for a bad crop if you had purchased the orchard on your own?"

Emily pulled out a folding chair and sat. "I figured I'd go back to restaurant work or hire out as a personal chef. Maybe even consult or give some cooking classes. Although there isn't nearly the demand for those services in Fredericksburg as there is here in the Dallas-Fort Worth area."

Dan wanted Emily to be happy—and if returning to her hometown to rear her child was the only way for her to do that, he would support her. "You could still do that."

Emily drummed her fingers on the tabletop. "But I wouldn't own the land. I wouldn't feel as secure." She opened her bag and pulled out the aforementioned contract. "The other thing that bothers me is the no-compete clause." She turned to the paragraphs she'd flagged.

Dan perused them with a critical eye. "Those are pretty standard."

Emily's slender shoulders sagged. "That's what my attorney said."

It was all Dan could do not to take her in his arms. "But?"

Emily squared her shoulders and sat back. "To not be able to work or purchase an orchard of my own anywhere in the state of Texas for two years, should our partnership dissolve, seems a little risky, too. What if I turn out to have my dad's ability to nurture an orchard and grow fruit? What if Tex and I just can't get along?" She exhaled. "What if a smaller place with a lot of potential comes along, and I decide my baby and I would be better off there? I wouldn't be able to act on it."

"You could ask to have the no-compete clause stricken. Or request Tex put in a salary for you to be deducted from your share of the profits."

"I know." Emily clamped her lips together.

Dan pulled out a chair and sat opposite her. "But you don't want to do that."

"I've thought about both things, of course."

He leaned toward her, forearms on the table. "And?"

She paused, looking even more distressed. "I think I'm just getting cold feet."

Dan studied the flush of color in her cheeks. "That happens to everyone who's trying to get a new venture off the ground," he soothed.

Emily put her elbow on the table and rested her chin on her upturned palm. "But what if it's more than that?" She sighed, looking more miserable than ever. "What if it's gut instinct telling me that going into partnership with an ex-fiancé is a mistake? What if I fail, the same way my mother did?"

Dan's instincts told him she would succeed, the way she'd succeeded in everything else on which she'd set her sights. She just needed reassurance, and the best way to do that was to approach it as methodically as she just had.

"First of all," he asked her bluntly, "do you still have feelings for Tex?"

"No."

"Does he appear to have feelings for you?"

Emily shook her head decisively. "No. Whatever we once had is long over."

"Then there shouldn't be any problem going into business together, at least from a romantic standpoint."

Which made Dan very glad.

"Second, from a grower's standpoint, you won't fail. You'll have Tex there to help you run that aspect of the operation."

"True. He's more than proved himself in the orchard business. He's a success three times over."

Dan took Emily's hand in his. The gesture was that of one friend to another, but to him it felt like much more. "The retail and tearoom business might be slower to build, but word of mouth is a powerful thing. So given your talent in the culinary arts, it's hard to imagine that not being a roaring success, too, especially considering the tourist trade in that part of the state every summer. Everyone needs a refreshing glass of iced tea."

Emily broke into a smile. "Or a soothing cup of hot."

He luxuriated in the silky warmth of her skin. "And some freshly churned peach ice cream or a peach sundae."

"Or peach cobbler or pie. And don't forget," Emily said, her eyes sparkling with building enthusiasm, "Tex's family property now features strawberries and blackberries, too. There are dozens of things we can make and sell, just with those three fruits."

"See?" Her happiness jump-started his. "You're already geared for success and you haven't even signed on the dotted line yet."

Finally relaxing, Emily kicked back in her seat. She studied him in consternation, then murmured in a tone laced with wonder, "You don't want me to do this and yet you're urging me on anyway."

Dan had promised himself he wouldn't be chivalrous to a fault again. Wouldn't accept a woman's excuses that anything was more important than the two of them—and the family they were trying to raise.

Yet here was Emily, who had one foot out the door, doing pretty much just that. And here he was, more into her than ever, saying, "I want all your dreams to come true, Emily." He squeezed her hand. *Whether they're my dreams or not.* "It's as simple—" *and complicated* "—as that."

THE NEXT FEW DAYS LOOKED to be incredibly busy and, Dan feared, a glimpse of the days to come. That evening, he missed his dinner because his consultation with the out-of-town clients went well over the allotted time and could not be rescheduled, as they were leaving the next morning. By the time he got home, the dishes were done and Emily was upstairs giving Ava an impromptu fashion consultation and co-reading a chapter of a Beverly Cleary novel with Kayla. Tommy wanted to talk to him about the praise he'd received from his wrestling coach about his victory in the previous night's match. By the time he had, Emily was on her way out the door.

Friday, Dan got home early, but Emily was late getting out of a last-minute gig she'd picked up. When she finally did arrive, the kids commanded every bit of her attention, and Dan was tapped to take Kayla to a birthday-party sleepover at the home of one of her friends. By the time he returned, the older kids had gone off to social engagements, and Emily had gone.

Saturday was a little better on his part. He was there when Emily arrived at four, looking incredibly pretty in an autumn-gold chef's coat, jeans and suede, knee-high boots. She had twisted her hair up in a messy knot on the back of her head. Her cheeks were full of color, her eyes bright and lively.

Once again, the kids preempted her attention the moment she walked in the door, her arms full of groceries for that night's dinner. They kept her occupied until they thanked her for the wonderful spaghetti supper and took off with Walt to go Christmas shopping for their mom's presents.

Happy to finally have a moment alone with Emily, Dan rolled up his sleeves. Her cheeks flushed from the heat of the kitchen, Emily lifted a staying hand. She sent him a look when he joined her at the kitchen sink. "Dishes are my job."

He squirted a dollop of soap into the empty pasta pot and added a stream of warm water. "I can help."

"The point is, Dan," Emily retorted gently, "you shouldn't have to."

But I want to, Dan thought, turning the warm water off. In fact, given his lack of contact with Emily the past few days, he'd take any reason to get close to her.

He studied her, too. He could see the shadows beneath her eyes. "You look tired."

Emily's breath left her body in a ragged sigh. She lounged against the cabinet. "Actually—" she reached up to catch her hair as it started to fall out of its clip "—I am. The past few days have been crazy!"

Dan scrubbed the inside of the pot and rinsed it clean. "What do you mean?"

Emily smiled again, although she was now looking slightly pale. She handed him a dish towel and stepped in front of the sink. "I've had twelve calls in two days for the not-quite-defunct Chef for Hire." She leaned over to put a dish in the dishwasher. "Everyone wants something done right away. It's almost like someone put the word out that I might not be leaving Fort Worth after all."

Here was his chance to tell her what he had done, Dan thought.

Not sure how she would take his less-than-selfless attempt to get her to reconsider leaving the city, Dan ignored the guilt tugging at him and let the chance to confess slide right on by. If Emily stayed, he reasoned silently, he could always tell her later. "What'd you do?"

"Well—" still leaning down, Emily struggled to fit the colander in the washer so it wouldn't bang against the plates "—given that no matter what I do I'm going to need a lot more money than I have right now, I accepted every gig, even the ones scheduled for December first and second."

Looking as if she'd straightened too abruptly, Emily braced one hand against the countertop.

Her cheeks, which had been so pale moments before, now turned a bright pink.

"With some caveats, of course." Her hand trembled slightly as she wiped down the counter where the stack of cleared plates had been. "I told my clients that I had to be out of my loft by then, so I'd have no cooking space of my own and would have to do absolutely all the prep work in their homes, but they were cool with that."

Resting a moment, Emily pressed the flat of her palm against her forehead.

"Anyway, between those twelve gigs and the eight nights I've got left working for you," she stated huskily, "I'll be in a lot better shape financially."

Wishing he could just order her to sit down, Dan again

studied Emily closely. "Should you be working that hard?" he asked, keeping his tone mild.

Seemingly irked, she dropped her hand from her forehead and turned her back to him. Shoulders stiff with defiance, she wiped the table. "I'm fine."

Deciding she needed to sit down and have a glass of ice water whether she wanted one or not, Dan set about making them both one. "How are the partnership negotiations going?" he asked casually.

Emily reached behind her for a chair. "Tex agreed to strike the no-compete clause," she reported as she started to pull the chair out with a trembling hand.

A little alarmed by the sudden grayish cast to her skin, Dan set the glasses down and circled around to assist. "That's good."

Emily took a deep breath and kept talking. "He hasn't agreed to give me an advance on profits via salary. He thinks he's taking enough of a risk and compensating me fairly as is." Her voice was now shaking as badly as her hand.

Dan slid an arm around her waist.

Rather than resist, Emily leaned helplessly into his touch. Another worrisome sign, Dan thought.

"I tried to talk to him about it—get him to see things from my perspective, but…." Emily's voice trailed off. Her lashes fluttered and her hand came up to touch her forehead again.

"Emily?" Dan said in concern.

And then she went limp.

Chapter Twelve

A gray mist swam in front of Emily's eyes. She heard Dan's voice rumble from a great distance away. Gradually it got closer. More distinct. Finally she was able to open her eyes, only to discover she was stretched out on the floor. He was kneeling beside her, cradling her head in his arms, a deeply concerned look on his handsome face. Still struggling to focus on her surroundings, she rasped, "Wh-what happened?"

"You fainted," Dan said.

The tenderness of his touch sent a river of warmth through her. She moaned, not sure whether she was more distressed or embarrassed. Weakly, she lifted her head and felt another tidal wave of wooziness wash over her. "I never faint," she told him with a scowl.

Dan's lips curved upward. "There's a first time for everything," he teased.

Grateful for his steady, reassuring presence—she would have been really frightened had he not been there with her—Emily moaned softly again and tried to sit all the way up. To her dismay, although she was feeling increasingly clear-headed in her thinking, she was still dizzy as all get-out.

Dan continued to hold her. "I'm taking you to the emergency room."

Had she not been pregnant, Emily would have argued. The fact that she was expecting a baby and so wanted to err on the side of safety had her insisting, "Let's call my obstetrician first."

Dr. Markham, it turned out, was already at the hospital checking on another patient. She told Dan she would meet the two of them in the emergency room.

When he hung up, Emily looked into Dan's eyes. Embarrassment heated her cheeks. "We're all going to feel very silly when we find out I simply fainted," she complained grumpily.

She trembled as Dan helped her to her feet. How easy it was to depend on him this way! she thought. "Like you said there's a first time for everything."

A first time for fainting. A first time for falling completely and hopelessly in love. And she was in love with Dan, Emily realized, as another wave of gratitude washed through her. Head over heels in love.

As they checked her in at the hospital, Dan asked, "Do you want me to go back with you or wait in the reception area?"

That, at least, was a remarkably simple decision. Emily had already had to weather far too much of this pregnancy on her own.

"Stay with me." She gripped his hand.

He looked into her eyes as if there was no place on earth he'd rather be. "Whatever you need," he told her quietly.

And Emily knew, in her soul, that he meant it. Just as she would do anything for him.

Her spirits soared as Dan took on the husband role as if they'd been married for years. He helped her undress and put on a hospital gown. Adjusted her pillows and drew the sheet over her. Then he stood by while Emily's obstetrician talked with Emily, checked her vitals and listened for the baby's heartbeat—which, to everyone's relief, came through strong and clear.

Happily, Dr. Markham agreed with Emily's assessment—she'd simply fainted. "It happens sometimes with pregnant women," Dr. Markham assured them both.

"Any particular reason why?" Dan asked, sounding more like an expectant father than a friend.

Dr. Markham looped her stethoscope around her neck. "When you're pregnant, your cardiovascular system undergoes significant changes. Sometimes that can leave you light-headed or a bit dizzy. These symptoms could be exacerbated if you stand up too quickly, haven't had enough food or drink or get overheated. Or even overdo things physically or feel anxious."

Well, that made sense, Emily thought, thinking she was guilty of not just one but all of the aforementioned causes.

Dr. Markham paused, pen poised over Emily's chart. "What were you doing when this happened?"

Emily swallowed. "I was working in the kitchen, talking with Dan."

Dr. Markham focused on the sudden tension in Emily's demeanor. "About what?" she asked.

Emily knew if her physician was to help her, she had to be completely honest. "Whether I should take on a business partnership with an old friend and move to Fredericksburg next month."

Dr. Markham and Emily had already discussed at length her situation and the decisions facing her. "Well, you know my feeling about that," the obstetrician said.

Emily nodded and repeated the gist of the aforementioned medical opinion. "Pregnancy and birth are momentous enough without adding the stress of a move or a job change. My being single makes that doubly so. I shouldn't do anything that isn't absolutely necessary until after the baby is born and I've adjusted to being a mom."

Until she'd become involved with Dan, Emily had felt buying the orchard was absolutely crucial to her happiness. Now she wasn't so sure. She still wanted to go *home*. But going back to the place where she'd grown up meant being without Dan and his family, and the challenge and comfort they brought to her life.

"Of course, it's not always possible to avoid such changes. But anytime a person can avoid making life harder than it needs to be…" Dr. Markham said with the practicality that had prompted Emily to choose her in the first place.

"They should." Emily smiled, taking the medical advice with the kindness and care with which it was given.

"But that said, if you decide you want to go ahead and move now, my staff and I will do everything we can to make sure the transition is a smooth one. Meantime—" Dr. Markham looked over Emily's chart "—you're due for an ultrasound soon, aren't you?"

Incredibly excited about that, Emily grinned. "I've got one scheduled for next week."

The doctor made a note. "Why don't we go ahead and do it now, since you're here."

It sounded good to Emily. And Dan would be here to see it, too. This pleased her more than she cared to admit.

Dr. Markham switched on the machine and smeared Emily's tummy with gel. As she moved the transducer over Emily's midriff, a black-and-white image of a baby appeared on the screen. The head and body were clearly visible. Dr. Markham showed them the baby's strongly pumping heart…the arms and legs…one tiny kicking foot, then another.

"Do you want to know the sex of the baby?" Dr. Markham said.

Too overcome with emotion to speak, Emily nodded.

"Congratulations, Mom. You're having a little girl."

The tears Emily had been holding back spilled over her cheeks and ran down her face. She was touched to see that Dan was just as choked up. Once again, it seemed they were sharing the joy of this pregnancy and the baby to come.

Dr. Markham took some measurements, noted them on the chart. "Everything looks great." She printed out a photo for Emily to take with her and handed it to her.

Emily stared at the filmy image of her baby, cozily curled up in her womb. She could see the side of her little girl's face and her tiny little body. She had a fist pressed nearly to her mouth, as if she was trying to figure out how to suck her thumb.

Dan stood next to Emily, studying the image, appearing equally transfixed. Instinctively he leaned closer, wrapping a protective arm about Emily's shoulders, drawing her even closer to his side.

Emily was suffused with warmth, inside and out. Overcome with feelings of love. This was her baby! Living, breathing, kicking inside her, evidence of the wonder of life.

Of hope.

Of love.

Of the beauty of the future.

Dr. Markham murmured something about discharge instructions, then ducked out of the exam room.

Emily and Dan exchanged emotional glances. Dan stroked her hair and looked into her eyes. Emily began to cry again. And this time, Dan didn't hesitate. He took her in his arms and held her close. "Congratulations, Mom," he said, sounding every bit as overcome with bliss as she was.

More than anything, Emily wished she could say, "Congratulations, Dad," to Dan. Her baby needed a daddy. Her baby needed *Dan* in her life, as much as Emily did. The question was, could that happen?

And *how* could it happen…if Emily were living a good four hours' drive away?

As if sensing something was wrong, Dan drew back. He cupped her face in his hand and tenderly wiped away her tears. His thumb stroking her cheek, he studied her expression. And in that second, as she felt the love and understanding simmering between them, Emily felt as if they were on the verge of an even bigger change. One that would transform both their lives.

But whatever Dan was about to say was cut off by the nurse who walked into the room and announced cheerfully, "Good news! Your posse has arrived!"

DAN WASN'T SURPRISED to see his entire family in the E.R. waiting room. He knew they cared about Emily. Even Walt had warmed up to her, not just as personal chef, but as an unofficial member of their tribe. Having seen the note Dan had left for them, they clearly wanted to show their support.

What was even more gratifying, though, was knowing how much Emily cared about them, too.

"Are Emily and the baby okay?" Ava jumped up as Emily and Dan walked over to them.

Tommy leaped out of his chair, too. "Why'd you faint?" he demanded protectively, moving around to study her face. "Is that *supposed* to happen?"

"We were worried!" Kayla dropped her coloring book and crayons long enough to declare.

Walt sized up Emily and added with gruff sincerity, "We hope everything is okay."

Emily beamed at the outpouring of love. "Everything's great," Emily told them, hugging each of the kids and finally Walt in turn.

Feeling happier than he had in a very long time, Dan explained, "The doctor did an ultrasound and Emily and the baby are fine."

Ava grinned slyly. "Did you find out what you're having?" she asked.

Tommy elbowed his older sister. "A baby, obviously," he joked, deadpan.

Ava rolled her eyes and elbowed Tommy right back. "I meant is it a boy or girl," she said.

Looking blissfully happy, Emily reached into her purse and pulled out the picture the doctor had printed out for them. Radiating pride, she announced softly to one and all, "It's a girl."

Aware he was as happy as he would be if this were his child they were talking about, Dan studied the black-and-white ultrasound photo of Emily's baby along with everyone else.

Finally Kayla tore her eyes away from the picture long enough to hug Emily. "What are you going to name her?" she asked, her chin resting on the curve of Emily's belly as she looked up.

Putting her arms around Kayla's shoulders in an instinctively gentle, maternal hug, Emily wrinkled her nose to demonstrate her own confusion. "I don't know yet." She grinned at Kayla, then looked around at the rest of the family to grin at them, too. "Maybe you all can help me come up with some names," she suggested.

The sense of family in the room deepened.

"That'll be fun," Ava declared.

"Awesome," Tommy agreed.

Already moving on to the next topic, Kayla tugged on Dan's jacket. "Daddy, did you ask her yet?"

Guilt flooded Dan. He hadn't had time to bring up the question the kids wanted the answer to.

Emily sent him a wordless, inquiring glance.

"We all agree. We really like having you around," Tommy said.

Ava nodded. "Life at our house is so-o-o much better since you started coming over to cook dinner for us."

"We want you to stay!" Kayla shouted.

"Whoa!" Dan said. "This isn't the time or place to be discussing Emily's plans."

The kids' shoulders slumped dispiritedly. Emily looked, curiously, just as wary of pursuing the matter as he was. Which, Dan guessed with disappointment, told him something he'd rather not know, too.

"The doctor wants Emily to go home and rest," he continued firmly, putting Emily's and her baby's health first and his own feelings aside.

Walt pulled out his car keys. "I'll get the kiddos home," he promised.

A round of congratulations and goodbyes ensued, complete with hugs and expressions of mutual relief that Emily and her baby were all right. Then Walt gathered up the family and departed while Dan drove Emily to her loft.

En route, he noted she was awfully quiet.

He wasn't sure what to say, either, after the unexpectedly eventful evening they'd had. He only knew he didn't want to do it while he was driving.

It was only when they got out of the car and he saw her in the glow of the streetlamps that he realized why she'd been silent.

"YOU'RE CRYING," DAN OBSERVED in dismay.

Emily turned her head away. Her steps graceful and deliberate, she headed for the front entrance to her building. "I'm just hormonal and overly emotional."

And if I believe that, Dan thought, *you probably have some prime swampland to sell me, too.*

Certain it was a heck of a lot more than hormones upsetting Emily, Dan fell into step behind her.

Pulse picking up, he watched the flash of her long legs and the sway of her slender hips. The funny thing was, he noted silently, Emily had no idea how sexy and appealing she was.

And he couldn't stop thinking about it.

Or how much he wanted her.

Not just as a lover and a friend—or a mother figure to his kids—but as an ongoing, integral part of his life.

The question was, how was he going to make that happen? Especially in the limited time they had left?

Drumming up more business for her hadn't helped. All that had done, he realized guiltily, was prompt more indecision and a fainting spell. Nor could he see himself standing in the way of her goal to return to Fredericksburg to rear her child.

Yet the critical thinker in him was sure there had to be

a solution to their mutual problem. A way for Emily to get everything she had ever wanted…and be with him, too.

He just had to put his thinking cap on and come up with it.

Meanwhile he could see that even though Emily had her face turned away from him, she was still silently weeping.

Determined to comfort her, he waited until they stepped into the elevator and the doors shut behind them before wrapping his arms around her and pulling her against him.

"I still want to know why you're crying," he murmured, burying his face in the softness of her hair.

Emily pushed him away. "I'm not! Not how you mean, anyway."

Dan was familiar with tears for no reason. These were not that, he was certain.

The elevator stopped at her floor and the doors slid open. He put a hand across the portal so she could exit safely. Then he stepped out, too, and fell into step beside her. He waited patiently as she unlocked the door to her loft, hit the lights and walked in. He followed.

Stunned, he looked around. The place was practically wall-to-wall moving boxes. Only a few clothes and cookbooks remained unpacked. The kitchen area, however, appeared to be fully functional. Probably because she still had catering gigs scheduled the next week.

Moving almost automatically, Emily shut the door behind them and turned the lock.

It wasn't quite the same as being officially invited in, but it was better than being escorted out, he decided, unable to help but notice how Emily was still surreptitiously wiping moisture from her cheeks.

"And furthermore," she continued, her temper rising, "a *gentleman* wouldn't have noticed!"

Dan teased her. "I thought we had established by now that where you're concerned, I'm no gentleman."

Emily slipped off her coat and pivoted to face him.

"Don't we both wish," she teased him right back. "But you *are* a gentleman. You caught me when I fainted, called my obstetrician, took me to the E.R., stayed with me and drove me home."

What he hadn't done, Dan realized, was throw caution to the wind and make love to her again, despite all the reasons they shouldn't.

"What are those—" Emily threw up her hands "—if not the actions of a gentleman?"

They were, Dan thought, the actions of someone who was very close to giving his heart away. For good this time.

But aware this might not be the moment to say that and have it received the way he wanted it received—with an open heart and mind—Dan said instead, "Those are the actions of someone who cares about you, Emily."

It wasn't what he wanted to say, but it was a start. And a start, he figured, was better than nothing.

Emily considered him for a moment and he was relieved to see that she'd stopped crying.

Her gaze meshed with his, she glided toward him. "You really mean that, don't you?" she asked, looking happier than she had all evening.

Dan couldn't lie about this. He took off his coat and dropped it over a chair. Emboldened by the desire he saw shining in her eyes, he swept her into his arms.

"I want to be part of you and your baby's life, Emily." He stroked a hand through her hair, pressed the other against her spine. "No matter where you ultimately decide to live. I want to know we can still see each other."

And Emily, it seemed, wanted and needed that, too.

"And still," Emily supposed out loud, searching his face and wreathing her arms about his neck, "do this…"

Their lips met. Dan meant to kiss her once, well, maybe two or three times, until she felt better and then call it a night. But the moment he felt her surrender in the way she opened her mouth to his, in the way she gave in to the passion with a soft sigh, all his patient, honorable intentions went by the wayside. Desire thundered through him, fueling a want and need that matched her own. The truth was, he wanted Emily. He'd wanted her every moment since the last time they'd made love. He just hadn't figured she would be up to it this evening. But up to it she was, as she put her all into the hot, searing kiss, intertwining her tongue with his. After stroking her hands up and down his back, she slipped them beneath his shirt to find the sensitive areas along his spine, between his shoulder blades, near his waist.

Blood thundered through him, pooling low. The urgency built, not just to make love to her, but to make her his. Not just for tonight, but for always.

And there was no doubt that she wanted him, too.

He unfastened the buttons on her shirt, slipped it off. Divested her of her jeans and boots, leaving her clad in just a pair of red-satin bikini panties that dipped beneath the sexy swell of her baby bump, and a matching satin bra that barely contained her swollen breasts. His body reacted to the sight of hers. He bent his head again and let the passion take hold.

Still kissing her rapturously, he pushed one strap off her shoulder, slowly, deliberately peeling the fabric down to expose the taut, rose-colored tip. Learning the shape of her, first by touch, then by sight and finally by taste, he luxuriated in the ripeness of her body. In the way she curled against him as her skin heated and trembled.

His own need building as surely as hers, he slipped a hand beneath her knees, lifted her and carried her over to her bed.

Gently he lowered her to the pillows. Turbulent need shimmering in her eyes, she lay on her side, her head propped up on her hand. She watched as he undressed and joined her there.

His need to protect her dictated he do everything with utmost tenderness and care. His desire to pleasure her made him prolong every touch, every caress, every kiss. Until there was no more waiting, only sweet, inevitable feeling as she tensed, shuddered and sighed.

Her body hot and trembling, she reached for him...

Emily had meant to take charge of their lovemaking this evening. To show Dan how wild and wicked and wonderful she could be. Instead, she'd ended up giving in to him, giving over. She had let him dominate, not just her body, but her heart and her soul. And maybe, she thought, her future, too.

But now it was her turn to explore. To learn his body anew, to let the silk of her hair tease the taut muscles of his abdomen and thighs. To stroke and tempt and tease as she took in the musky masculine scent of him. She tasted the salt of his perspiration and the familiar sweetness of his skin. Aware she had never felt more alive, so safe, so loved, so protected, she soared toward the ultimate closeness. Yet still she focused on one seductive plateau after another until he, too, could stand it no more. With a groan that was part contentment, part need, he shifted upward. Sat back against the headboard and pulled her astride his lap.

Emily wound her arms about his neck and shoulders while Dan grasped her by the hips. Their bodies came together as one.

Aware nothing had ever felt so good or so right, Emily melted into his touch. She let him show her the way and set the pace…until there was no holding back the passion roaring through her…no containing the love in her heart. Together they skyrocketed into ecstasy, became suspended in tender fulfillment. And then drifted slowly, inevitably down.

Still shuddering with the aftershocks, Emily molded her body to his and pressed her breasts against the steely muscles of his chest. She clung to him, savoring the moment and the man. She thought about what had happened as he stroked a hand through her hair. Not just tonight, but every time they were alone together—and even when they weren't.

She had tried so hard to deny it, but there was no getting around it—there was something special here. Something she had never felt before and was certain she would never feel again with anyone else. The urge to go back to the past and bring new life to the orchard her family had built paled in comparison to her desire to build a family with Dan. She could pretend she still wanted to bring up her child alone. That it would be enough.

Or she could be honest with herself—and Dan.

Holding as tightly to the burst of unexpected courage as she was to the feelings of well-being their lovemaking had engendered, Emily drew back far enough to look into Dan's eyes. Her voice soft, she threw caution to the wind and told him what had been in her heart for some time. "I want to be your lover, Dan, as well as your friend. And I want you to be mine."

Dan's brow furrowed.

Clearly, Emily thought, this was not what Dan had been expecting to hear. She hadn't anticipated saying it, either. She held up a hand before he could respond. "I know it's not the usual thing for a woman in my condition to ask. And that you might not want to commit to something like that for even the duration of my pregnancy…" She trailed off.

Dan bent his head and kissed her, and the kiss felt like a commitment, like a bridge to their future. "Consider us exclusive," he murmured, smiling. "Starting now."

And then, just so she would know how serious he was, he kissed her with an intensity that took her breath away and made sweet, tender love to her all over again.

Chapter Thirteen

"I wish I didn't have to go home," Dan admitted an hour later as he climbed out of Emily's bed.

Emily turned on her side to watch him gather his clothes. "But if you don't, they'll likely assume something else is wrong with me or the baby."

When instead, Dan thought with contentment, everything was very right.

"Speaking of which—" he pulled on his boxers and jeans and sat down beside her on the bed "—we never really had a chance to talk about the discharge instructions the nurse gave you."

Emily made a face. "You mean the ones about making sure I'm not working too many hours and am taking care of myself?"

"Those would be the ones."

There was a brief silence as Emily ran her palm over the sheet with the same deliberation she used when she made love to him. She lifted her gaze to his. "You think I've been working too hard, don't you?"

"Honestly? Yes," he said somberly.

Emily sighed and rolled over onto her back. She drew

the sheet over the full, womanly curves of her breasts and folded one arm behind her head. The other rested against her brow, shielding her gaze from view. "It's occurred to me, too," she said on a disgruntled sigh.

Dan lifted her hand and kissed the inside of her wrist. "You've looked tired ever since you took on extra gigs."

Emily's lips twisted ruefully. "I've *felt* tired." Her breasts rose and lowered with each long, slow breath. "Between that and all the packing and the stress of trying to negotiate a satisfactory partnership agreement with Tex, it's clear to me I haven't been getting enough rest."

More than ever, Dan found himself wanting to be the one who took care of her and looked out for her. "So what are you going to do about it?" he asked gently, deciding this time he would not stand by idly while it all fell apart. He'd find a way to help Emily and himself gain everything they wanted and needed, even if it meant he had to think outside the box.

Emily shrugged, her worry fading as quickly as his intensified. "I guess I'm going to have to start putting my feet up a little more. Probably stop taking on any more extra work until I do move."

There it was again, the elephant in the room. "And until then?" It was with effort that Dan kept his voice mild.

An emotion he couldn't decipher simmered in her eyes. "I've got one or two jobs a day in addition to making dinner for your family."

Dan wrapped his arms around her and brought her close. "Do you want to stop cooking for us?" He planted a kiss in her hair.

Emily shook her head adamantly, trailing her fingers over his pecs. "I don't want to let the kids down."

"Do you want to give up any of the others?"

She sighed. "Nope."

A frayed silence fell between them.

"I'm a working mom, Dan," she reminded him with a deeply disappointed look.

He made no response. How many times had his ex-wife said the same thing while running herself ragged?

Emily promised in a flat, nonnegotiable tone, "I'll figure it out."

Brenda had said that, too. Only there had never been enough time for family, Dan recalled sadly, never enough time for the two of them. Were he and Emily headed down the same path? And if so, would she end up hurting not just him and his family, but herself and her baby, too?

Or was Emily smarter and better able to compromise?

There was no way to tell as her chin took on that stubborn tilt he knew so well. "I'll work everything out, Dan," she repeated. "I'll find a way to be together with you that won't take away from anyone or anything else important."

Looking into her eyes, seeing the fire of her ambition—and the depth of her determination to be with him and his kids—Dan could almost believe Emily would somehow manage to have it all. Unfortunately he knew how difficult a goal like that was to achieve, especially when the over-extended person in question was determined to continue going it alone in the decision-making process.

It wasn't that Emily didn't care what he thought or felt. She'd made it clear in the way she interacted with him and his family that she did. But this was all new territory for her. Maybe if she'd had experience juggling the demands of a relationship, kids and work, she would have under-stood the hardships of what they were facing.

Unfortunately Dan knew all too well what the odds were of their union succeeding within the parameters Emily was contemplating. Bitter experience with his own family had taught him that good intentions were a dime a dozen. *Wanting* to be with loved ones wasn't enough. For it all to work, sacrifices had to be made.

Speaking of which…

He had a major forfeiture coming up. And like it or not, so did she.

"About my family and the upcoming holiday—" Dan began.

Emily lifted a silencing hand, cutting him off. She sat up in bed, her knees drawn to her chest. "I'm with you."

That was interesting, Dan thought, since *he* barely knew what he was going to say.

Emily clasped her arms around her upraised knees and continued with heartfelt emotion, "I know it's going to be a complicated week, Dan. But I'm ready for it."

The question was, Dan wondered, was *he?*

"Holidays have been tough at my house since the divorce," he said. "Actually," he corrected, "they were tough before then, since there was always a lot of disarray and disconnection in the household."

"I know," Emily said sympathetically, regarding him with kind eyes and a soothing smile. "I guessed as much." She reached over to clasp his hand in hers, the warmth of her fingers as gentle as her voice. "And the truth is, holidays can be a lot to handle for everyone, even when everything in the family is 'normal.'"

"Go on," he said quietly.

Her lips twisted ruefully again. "I've certainly worked enough of them as a chef, seen how people interact when under stress." She sighed. "And in extreme cases like mine, where I'd lost both my parents—or in the case of your kids, who are still dealing with their mom's habitual absence and the fallout from the divorce—the pressure of those special occasions is even worse."

"I just don't want anyone to be disappointed," he admitted.

She squeezed his hand. "Believe me, I understand, with Thanksgiving now only five days away and Brenda arriving, that you and I are going to have to do what is best for the family and put our own needs on a back burner." She locked gazes with him. "I get that you and I are not going to have any time alone together. And I want you to know it's okay."

Had Dan harbored any doubt about the generosity of her spirit, it would have disappeared in that instant.

It was his own selfish nature, he realized, that bore closer examination. He was tired of hiding his feelings. Tired of having to disavow the best thing that had ever happened to him. Tired of basically lying to everyone around them.

"We don't have to hide in the shadows," he said. "We can let my family know that we're…friends, and we're spending time together."

Emily studied him for a long silent, moment. "You really want to do that?" she asked finally.

He really did.

She, however, clearly did not, if the frown tugging at the corners of her mouth was any indication.

Dan pushed on in an attempt to persuade her. "I don't really see that we have much choice unless we want to wait until we're confronted. Probably at some very inopportune time." Dan shrugged. "I can tell from some of the looks I'm getting that Walt has already guessed we're—"

"An item?" Emily interrupted wryly.

Dan had been about to call it something a whole lot more romantic. But he was glad he hadn't. He sensed he was pushing her too hard, too fast, as it was. "Correct," he confirmed. "And the kids aren't far behind."

"The point is," she said, "they haven't brought it up, and given the complicated nature of the holiday, I don't think we should, either." She paused. "Our relationship is too new, too special. I don't think anyone should know about us just yet."

"So you want to just get through the week," Dan surmised. Although it was hard to contain his disappointment, he knew it would probably be best to proceed with caution.

Emily nodded. "And see where we go from there."

"I DON'T KNOW HOW TO thank you," Brenda Kingsland said the following Thursday afternoon as she and Emily lingered over coffee in the formal dining room. They were enjoying the peace and quiet while Dan, Walt and the kids dealt with the dishes in the kitchen. Emily had been given a reprieve because she had cooked the meal, and Brenda had been spared because she was a guest. And, as had been proved repeatedly during the past four days, because she was inept when it came to anything domestic.

"This has been the best Thanksgiving ever," Brenda continued with what appeared to be real contentment.

Emily was quick to agree.

She hadn't known what to expect when Dan's ex-wife had arrived in town on Monday for a week-long holiday. Certainly not that she and Brenda would forge an easy friendship. But that was exactly what had happened.

Emily smiled at the tall, lithe physician with the deeply

tanned skin and pronounced crow's feet around her eyes. Brenda was dressed in her usual outfit of loose-fitting khaki trousers and shirt and sturdy lace-up hiking boots. Her long, silvery-blond hair was plaited in a single braid. Her nails were short. And her makeup was nonexistent.

The only flaw Emily could see in Dan's strikingly beautiful ex-wife was that she was so tied to her work, she was often oblivious to everything else. She was frequently on the phone or the computer, conferring with colleagues halfway around the world, rendering both medical opinions and managerial advice.

Fortunately, due to the time difference, she did a lot of her work at night and so could spend a lot of time getting caught up with her three children, to their continuing delight.

"Glad I could help," Emily said in response to Brenda's compliment.

Brenda slid the BlackBerry from her pocket and checked for messages. She read quickly, then typed in a response, before pocketing the phone once again. Leaning back in her chair, she sipped her coffee contentedly. "I can't get over the difference in the kids. In the past when I've come home, they've been moody and resentful to the point I'd begun to think it might be better if I just stayed away entirely." She beamed. "But this time they've been really glad to see me, almost relaxed. Dan, too. And that was a surprise. Usually he's tense and irritable. We all are."

She flashed Emily a grateful look. "It's obviously helped, having you around. Making everything run smoothly, reminding us through your own example that we don't need everything society says we do to be happy, that we can get by simply by focusing on what we *most* need." Brenda summed up thoughtfully, "In your case, a baby. In Dan's, a normal family life. And in mine, the knowledge I'm bringing medical care to people in desperate situations."

There was no doubt, Emily thought, that Brenda was not only a very talented physician, but a noble one.

She imagined that chivalrous streak was one of the things that had brought Dan and Brenda together, even as their vastly different goals and dreams had torn them apart. To the point now that not even a hint of sexual chemistry remained between the two of them. They were like distant relations, who while still having the power to get under each other's skin, mostly had no real reaction to each other at all. Hard to imagine they had once lived together and had three children together, whom they both clearly loved.

Knowing it was none of her business, Emily found herself asking curiously, "Do you ever regret the divorce?"

Brenda's reaction was automatic. "No. Dan and I were never all that good together." Brenda grimaced. "Never really on the same page. If it weren't for the intense passion we had in the very beginning and the fact that we had kids we both cared about, we never would have stayed together as long as we did." Brenda made a face. "Dan doesn't do well with long-distance relationships."

Which doesn't bode well for me, Emily thought nervously.

"He tried. We both did. But he's a man who needs a woman around. Not—" Brenda took another long sip of coffee "—a wife who is off on a mission."

Without warning, the kids came back into the living room.

Kayla skidded to a halt next to Brenda. The eight-year-old hugged her mother exuberantly. "Okay, Mom, the dishes are all done! So you can tell us where you're taking us for Christmas now!"

PANDEMONIUM REIGNED for the next two hours. Finally Walt's SUV was packed with suitcases and skis, and Walt, Brenda and the kids headed for the Dallas-Fort Worth airport in plenty of time to make their 7:30 p.m. flight to Colorado.

After four days of constant activity, respective work demands and time with family, Emily and Dan were finally alone.

Emily savored the realization, her spirits lifting even as her body sagged with the fatigue of a long and demanding week.

She turned away from the front windows and saw Dan watching her with the affection he no longer had to hide. Relaxing, she let her feelings for him show, too.

They linked hands and made their way into the living room, where they sank onto the sofa. Dan draped his arm over her shoulders, and Emily nestled into the welcoming curve. She thought about all the surprises the week had brought, then asked, "Did you know that Brenda planned to surprise Walt and the kids with a ski trip?"

He'd certainly been warmly enthusiastic. But they were *his* kids, too, and it was a holiday weekend, a long one at that. Emily wasn't sure how Dan felt about being left behind.

Dan shifted, then pulled Emily onto his lap. "She didn't share that with me, but I can't really say I'm surprised." He put one arm around Emily's waist, threaded the other through her hair, stroking softly.

He continued matter-of-factly, "We all love to ski. It's a great gift and an easy way for them to celebrate an early Christmas—especially since the resort is providing an already-decorated suite complete with tree. The only downside is that the kids won't get back here until late

Sunday evening, which will make getting up for school tough on Monday morning. But I'm sure they'll manage."

Emily flattened her palm against the center of his chest and felt the strong, steady beat of his heart. "What about you?" She noted how delicate her hand looked against his broad, muscular chest. "Are you sorry you're not going?"

"No," Dan said sincerely. He captured her hand in his and rubbed his lips sensually over her knuckles. Then he entwined their fingers and smiled down at her. "Brenda needs time alone with the kids. I want her to have as much as possible."

As usual he was generous to a fault, Emily thought.

"It's just too bad you and I both have to work this weekend," he continued.

Emily's brow furrowed. She shifted around slightly, her bottom rubbing across the hard muscles of his lap. "I knew *I* had one last gig tomorrow," she murmured. "But I didn't know *you* had to work." Didn't most businesses—like Dan's architectural firm—take the day after Thanksgiving off?

Abruptly Dan's expression closed. "There's a prospective client I have to see."

"I'll be done by around four tomorrow afternoon," Emily said.

"I'm not sure how long my meeting will go," Dan said evasively. Taking her by the hand, he led her toward the stairs.

But until then, he knew exactly what he wanted to do. And Emily did, too...

"ARE YOU SURE THIS IS A GOOD idea?" Grady asked Dan as the group gathered in the unfinished atrium of One Trinity River Place.

"I know you want her to stay," Travis added. "But excluding Emily this way..."

"Emily's had enough stress the last few weeks as it is," Dan said. To the point that the accumulation of fatigue and anxiety had made her faint.

He thought about how exhausted she'd looked the night before, how she'd fallen asleep in his arms immediately after they'd made love.

"Still," Jack cautioned, "if there's one thing I remember well about being married, it's that women like to be *consulted....*"

"And Emily will be," Dan said firmly, "just as soon as I know there is actually something to consult her about."

Nate rubbed his jaw with the flat of his hand, his expression skeptical. "I hope you know what you're doing," he told Dan finally.

Dan did. He looked at his friends. "Emily doesn't want to leave Fort Worth."

"You mean *you* don't want her to leave," Travis corrected.

"She'd be better off here," Dan insisted stubbornly. "Even her obstetrician thinks so."

"Don't you think that's for her to decide and not you?" Grady argued back.

"The reason she wants to leave is that she doesn't think there is any way she can successfully restore her family's orchard business and still be here in Fort Worth."

"She might have a point there," another voice said dryly.

All five men turned.

The interloper extended a hand and said gruffly, "Let's get started, shall we?"

EMILY COULDN'T BELIEVE it was working out this way. She and Dan *finally* had a chance to enjoy an entire weekend alone together, and they'd barely seen each other. He was gone when she'd woken up Friday morning. She'd called him at noon, but he wasn't answering his cell. By the time he returned her phone call, she was working and couldn't answer him. She thought they'd be together Friday evening. Wrong again. He and the partners of One Trinity River Place were all deep in the middle of some mysterious negotiations that were set to go all through the dinner hour. Emily offered to cook for them—no charge—but Dan had turned her down, saying it was already taken care of.

Trying not to feel hurt he had selected someone other than her to cater the meal, she'd spent the evening finishing up her packing. Saturday morning, she'd been busy supervising the emptying out of her loft and the loading of her belongings onto the moving truck so they could be taken to storage.

She'd thought Dan might come over or at least offer to help with that. He hadn't. Nor had he shown up for lunch. Or been able to meet her for the afternoon movie she'd been dying to see.

Finally, around four-thirty, he called her and asked her to come down to One Trinity River Place to give her opinion on something.

Hardly the romantic date she'd been hoping for.

But he sounded both insistent and oddly formal in his request, so she agreed and drove there to meet him.

He was waiting by the security gate of the twelve-foot-high steel fence that enclosed the construction site, talking with the last person in the world she would have expected to see.

Heart thrumming in her chest, Emily moved forward and extended her hand. "Hello, Tex…Dan." She greeted both with the same careful politeness Dan had used on the phone with her. "What are you doing here?" The question was directed at Tex.

Tex exchanged glances with Dan. "I wanted to talk to you," he said in an all-business tone.

Emily knew her ex-fiancé could be pushy when it came to getting what he wanted, but this crossed over the line. "Our meeting with the attorney isn't until Monday afternoon," she reminded Tex. And although after weeks of indecision, she now knew exactly what she was going to say at that meeting, she didn't want to have that conversation now…and she didn't want to have it with Dan present.

"Actually," Dan interjected smoothly, with a convivial look from Tex, "we'd both like to talk with you."

The weekend took yet another surreal turn.

"Why don't we go inside," Dan suggested.

Feeling at a distinct disadvantage regarding whatever was going on here—and clearly there was something going on—Emily fell into step between the two men. She'd been shut out of some major decision-making when she'd been engaged to Tex. She'd never expected to be similarly shut out by Dan. But to her consternation, that was exactly what seemed to be happening.

The three of them walked in silence across the roughly paved lot and into the beautifully designed stone-and-glass building. Along the way, more than one surreptitious glance was exchanged between the two men.

Finally Emily'd had enough of it. Hands in the pockets of her jacket, she swung around to square off with them. "One of you better tell me what is going on."

"Dan came to me with a business proposal," Tex said. "And it's a good one."

For the next few minutes Emily listened in numb disbelief. At last Tex and Dan finished talking. Still thrown for a loop, she decided to recap, just to make sure she understood the plan that had been developed completely in her absence. "So what you're proposing, Tex, is that you and I go into partnership together, but instead of me being caretaker of the orchard in Fredericksburg, I live here in Fort Worth."

"And oversee the building of the new retail store for all of Tex's orchards," Dan said, "and the adjoining tearoom, which will both be located on the first floor of One Trinity River Place."

"Obviously we'll need to go over the details," Tex said, "and we can do that on Monday afternoon when we meet with the lawyer about our partnership agreement. But I wanted to be here when Dan first broached the subject with you," Tex said. "Just to be sure you knew I was fully on board with this. And have been since Dan and the other guys and I first started meeting yesterday morning."

Still feeling a little like she'd been run over by a Mack truck, Emily signaled her comprehension with a slight nod of her head.

"Anyway, as I told Dan, I've got to get going." Tex paused to shake hands with Dan. "But we'll talk Monday, okay, Emily?"

"We certainly will." Doing her best to control her turmoil, Emily offered a tight smile.

Thinking the matter settled, Tex strode off.

Dan and Emily faced each other in the empty building.

How had it happened? she wondered as the enormity of her mistake hit her full force. She'd done it again, come into a family's home as a personal chef. Only this time, instead of just becoming way too emotionally attached to the kids and even the crusty great-uncle who lived with them, she'd fallen in love with their dad.

Very unwisely, it seemed, since Dan clearly did not understand how much she feared turning into an overly dependent woman like her mother, who leaned on the man in her life for the solution to every problem. And if Dan didn't know that, if he didn't recognize her as the savvy and strong single mom-to-be that she was, then he didn't know her at all! Clearly, she thought ominously, he wanted to mold her into the kind of woman he wished he'd had in his life all along.

"Well?" Dan asked finally, with an arch of his brow. "What do you think?"

Emily glared back. *"How could you?"* she said.

Chapter Fourteen

"What do you mean, how could I?" Dan retorted, not sure why she wasn't happy about what he'd done.

Okay, so maybe his proposal hadn't included her dream of living in the place where she had grown up, but surely she had to see that was no longer possible—if the two of them were to be together. His business was here in Fort Worth. So was Chef for Hire, which she'd yet to let go of. He had kids in school. A home big enough for all of them when they married, as he was sure they eventually would. Hopefully before the baby was born. And it wasn't as if he'd asked her to give up her dream of restoring the orchard business her father had started. He had found a way for her to participate in that—even more lucratively, too! As for being in Fredericksburg, they could always visit and stay in one of the nice hotels or bed-and-breakfasts in the area.

Emily had to know all this, too. Yet she was staring at him like he'd betrayed her in the worst possible way. "You went behind my back!"

Dan clenched his jaw. He wasn't going to apologize for fighting to give their relationship the best possible chance of succeeding, for doing what would make everyone as happy as possible. "Only because I didn't want to present you with you an option and get your hopes up with a plan that turned out not to be viable," he said. "And frankly, before yesterday, I wasn't sure Tex would go for my idea at all."

Emily folded her arms, her expression militant. "But he did."

The sarcasm in her voice rankled. Knowing what was at stake, Dan worked to contain his own temper. "Tex saw the business benefits of putting a retail store for all of his orchards in downtown Fort Worth. Plus, by leasing space on the ground floor, the two of you can have it built to your specifications, instead of going to the trouble of converting a barn. You can open the store in a few months instead of six and stay in Fort Worth. You can have your baby here."

Dan's smile broadened as he thought about how much he'd managed to arrange on her behalf by calling in favors and leaning on his friends. "And even lease one of the residential units on the upper floors for as long as you want, at the business-tenant discount, which will make commuting to work a snap."

Emily shook her head in a parody of being impressed. "You've thought of everything," she murmured.

"I've tried," Dan said. He stepped closer and took her rigid body in his arms.

Emily's eyes darkened. "Except one thing," she said with an icy hauteur that would have sent a lesser man running for the exit.

"What's that?"

Angrily she shoved away from him. "I could never be with a man who disrespected me so thoroughly!" she fumed.

Dan stared at Emily. "Disrespected you," he echoed, stunned. "How the hell have I done that?"

"By not including me in any of this!"

He stared at her in frustration. "I told you my reasons," he reminded her impatiently.

"I know," she scoffed. "You wanted to protect me."

He felt a growing sense of helplessness. "You've been under a lot of stress—as your recent fainting episode and visit to the E.R. proved."

She angled her chin at him. "I'm fine."

"For the moment," he muttered.

"And," Emily countered, her eyes glittering, "I would have continued to be fine had you chosen to talk to *me,* instead of Tex, about your plans!"

Unlike Emily, Dan did not consider his desire to protect his woman from unnecessary stress to be a character flaw. "I'm talking to you now," he said, pushing the words through his teeth.

"After the fact."

He tried to reason with her one last time. "I wouldn't be doing any of this if I didn't respect you," he said quietly.

"Respect me or want to keep sleeping with me?" Her low voice reverberated with hurt and disillusionment. She stared right through him. Her voice was shrill, angry and very sad. "Face it, Dan. You want me here because you don't do well at long-distance relationships."

Her accusation hit him where it hurt. "I'm not going to deny I think they are doomed to fail," he said straightforwardly. "Two people can't build anything lasting if they are never physically together."

"So you came up with a plan to keep us in close proximity."

Feeling more resentful with every second that passed,

Dan warned, "I'm not going to apologize for wanting to be close enough to be a part of you and your baby's life, and have you be a part of mine."

Emotion choked her throat. "You seriously don't think you did anything wrong here?" she whispered, aghast.

How could he? When everything he'd done had been because he wanted their relationship to have the best possible chance to succeed. He shrugged and confessed flatly, "I seriously don't."

They stared at each other, neither giving ground.

Emily sighed, looking as if her heart were broken. And Dan knew it was over even before she walked away.

"IT'S NOT LIKE WE DIDN'T TRY and tell you it was a mistake," Grady told him that evening as the men all gathered at Dan's home for an impromptu bull session.

Grady opened up five bottles of beer as Travis plated pizza, Jack divvied up the wings and Nate grabbed a roll of paper towels to use as napkins.

Dan switched on the big-screen TV and turned the channel to the Dallas Cowboys football game. With Walt and the kids still in Aspen with his ex-wife and Emily absent, his house was impossibly lonely.

Even if his family had been there, Dan thought on a disgruntled sigh, it still would have been empty without Emily.

How had she become such a big part of his life so quickly?

And why was she being so unreasonable? Didn't she feel as deeply about him as he did about her?

Was it all about needing a man during this momentous time in her life and he just happened to be there? Had she been seduced by the vision of a big, close-knit family as much as by him? Or was it something more along the lines of what his ex had felt, that being with Dan—and the rest of the family—was just not ever going to be enough to make her want to stay and sign on for a lifetime of bliss?

Aware the guys were waiting for some explanation, Dan shrugged. "I'd like to think her unreceptive reaction was the result of pregnancy hormones."

"Face it," Grady said. "You screwed up by not including her in the development of the alternative business plan."

Guilt warred with hurt pride. "I was trying to protect her!" he argued.

"Women don't want to be protected—they want to be included," Travis stated.

So Emily had said, Dan reflected as his friends chowed down. "That's still no reason for her not to forgive me," he grumbled.

"You have to give her time," Nate said.

Dan didn't think time was going to make a bit of difference. He'd seen the disgusted way Emily looked at him before she'd marched off in stormy silence.

Dan continued to defend himself. "It's not as if I set out to hurt her."

"No, just rearrange her life," Grady noted.

Dan looked over at his friend. The McCabe men were known for their way with the opposite sex.

"Maybe it's not what you were offering her so much as what you *weren't*," Travis speculated.

Dan set his untouched plate on the coffee table in front of him. "Speak English," he commanded.

"You're asking her to deep-six her plans to move to Fredericksburg and stay here," Travis concluded as if the problem with that was obvious.

And it seemed to be, Dan thought, to everyone in the room but him.

"And yet from what I can tell," Travis continued sagely, "you haven't offered her anything else that really matters."

The heck he hadn't! Dan thought. "I want to be part of her and her baby's life." In his book that was no small pledge.

"And that makes you different from everyone else in her realm in what way?" Jack asked in his usual linear-thinking way.

"I'm sure lots of people have offered to help her when the baby is born." Grady peered at Dan, considering. "Why did you go so completely over the top to make sure she stayed in Fort Worth?"

Nate jumped in with *his* two cents. "And more important, if you expect her to say yes and do what you want, what are you going to give her that no one else can?"

IT WAS INCREDIBLE, EMILY thought on Sunday afternoon, how cold and empty the loft felt with all her stuff gone, save for one small suitcase and a few cleaning supplies. Incredible to think that life, which had seemed so perfect yesterday, was now one giant mess of lost hopes and dreams.

She filled the bucket with warm water and cleanser. Set it on the floor. Lowered the mop and then stopped as the buzzer sounded.

Unfortunately it wasn't the visitor she'd hoped to see. But one she needed to talk to nevertheless.

"Hello, Tex," Emily said a moment later, ushering him in.

He shoved his hands in his pockets as she resumed mopping the floor. "Dan told me what happened. I wasn't sure you'd still be speaking to me."

"To either of you," Emily corrected.

Tex stepped to the left of the cleaning. "Look, just because Dan had an idea—which was a great one, by the way—and I concurred with him, doesn't make our idea wrong."

That was the hell of it, Emily thought. Moving the retail business and tearoom to Fort Worth was a great idea. She wished she'd thought of it! "It doesn't make the way you went about it right, either," she pointed out grumpily.

Tex shrugged in concession, moving once again. He watched as she dipped the mop back in the bucket of sudsy water and worked the lever that wrung out the excess moisture. Finished, she slapped the mop back down on the floor.

Tex exhaled and tried again. "Okay, so I had an inkling you'd be ticked off."

And hence had known not to do it, but had gone ahead anyway, just as he had when they'd been engaged in what seemed like light-years ago, Emily thought.

"I also agreed with Dan that there was no point in getting you all excited about something if the business case wouldn't support it." Tex defended himself in the same straight-talking way Dan had. "And since Dan and his friends had one set of information, me another, it made sense for us all to talk before taking things any further." Tex lifted a hand before she could interrupt. "In retrospect, I get that we should have included you from the very beginning of the idea stage, Emily. Frankly, I'm sorry we didn't. But it doesn't *change* the bottom line."

"And that is?"

"Dan had one heck of an innovative idea that could stand to net you and me both a handsome income for years to come. If he went about it the wrong way, so be it. It doesn't mean your friendship with him, if that's all it is—and I'm thinking it's a helluva lot more than that—has to end." Tex paused. "So what's really going on here, Emily?" he asked. "What exactly has you running scared? And why won't you do what you usually do with a problem, which is face it head-on?"

Because, Emily thought, *I'm scared. The stakes are too high.*

But, her more rational self argued, weren't they just as high—if not higher—if she did nothing?

She'd been so very close to getting what she really wanted. What she had always wanted.

"Life takes detours, Emily," Tex said quietly.

Emily knew where this heading. "It's what happens—" she used a popular cliché "—when you're making other plans."

"It doesn't mean that what you want is out of reach. Especially now."

Emily thought about what Tex had said all the way to her hotel. By the time she checked in, she knew what she had to do.

DAN HAD JUST CARRIED the boxes of Christmas lights out of the garage when Emily turned her van into his driveway.

Stunned by how hungry he was for the sight of her, he let his eyes rove over her. She wore a red turtleneck sweater and a black leather jacket. Her glossy dark hair fell over her shoulders in loose disarray. Her lips were a soft cranberry-red, her expression…tense.

He wondered if she had come by to tell him she quit and collect the cooking utensils she'd left at his house. Or if she was going to give him another chance. Her brief glance, as she slid out from behind the wheel and shut the door, gave no clue.

Pulse thundering, he straightened and met her halfway.

In a drift of soft, sexy perfume, she looked up at him. He looked down at her. Without a word, she went up on tiptoe, wrapped her arms around his neck and pressed her lips to his.

Surprise shot through Dan, along with a healthy dose of desire. He kissed her the way he'd been wanting to kiss her for what seemed like forever. She kissed him back in exactly the same way, then ever so slowly disengaged. "I thought we should get that out of the way," she said in a careful, neutral tone that had him wondering if that had been an I-want-to-make-up-with-you kiss or a goodbye kiss. She took his hand in hers, held it firmly. "I also really think we should talk."

Dan nodded. It wasn't like him to let the woman in his life take the lead, especially in a situation like this, where things could easily go the wrong way. But after all that had happened, he figured he should let Emily call the shots, if only to show her how much he respected her feisty, independent nature. "Living room?" he suggested.

"How about the kitchen?" she returned, looking more coolly determined than he had ever seen her.

Hand in hand, they headed for the coziest room in the house—at least since *she* had been there. She moved to the stove and put the kettle on to boil. Her lips twisted in a rueful line. "I've been doing a lot of thinking."

"So have I." *About you. And life. And family. And everything we could still have...*

Emily swallowed and looked him in the eye. "If the offer to continue to cook for your family is still open," she said quietly, "I'd like to take it."

Her proposal wasn't what he'd been anticipating. But it was a step in the right direction of getting her back in his life. "For as long as you want," Dan agreed huskily.

"But only on one condition," she amended, and his heartbeat picked up.

Dan lifted his hands in surrender. "Name it."

She paused. "I don't want to be paid."

Dan let that sink in. "I'm not sure how I feel about that," he said finally. "It's a lot of work."

Emily took both his hands in hers. "It's become a labor of love. And I don't want to be doing it as an employee of your family any longer. I want to be doing it as a, well, friend."

Dan's heart sank.

He'd been hoping for much more than that.

He'd also promised himself he wouldn't leap ahead or steer her anywhere she wasn't ready to go. Not this time. With effort he held himself back.

Her eyes began to sparkle. Tilting her head to one side, she continued in a low tone laced with mischief, "And I know how you like to think outside the box."

He chuckled ruefully. "My habit of doing that seems to have gotten me in pretty big trouble the last few days."

Emily tugged him close. "Trouble can be good."

Trouble with Emily felt very good. Still, Dan didn't want to jump the shark again. Delighting in the warmth of her body, pressed against his, he rested his hands on her waist. "What are you saying?"

"Quite simply—" her voice suddenly sounded as emotional as he felt "—that I love you." She drew in a jerky breath. "I've been in love with you for a while now—I just was afraid to admit it to myself and to you."

Even though Dan understood, he had to know. "Why?" He eyed her determinedly.

Trembling, Emily splayed her palms across his chest. "Because it scares me," she whispered. "I've never wanted anything or anyone as much as I want a life with you."

Happiness welled up inside him. Aware Emily's eyes weren't the only ones that were getting wet, he admitted gruffly, "I feel the same way." Kissing her sweetly, he murmured, "I love you, Emily, so much."

She held him tight. "Which is why you went to so much trouble to find a way for us to be together."

He stroked a hand tenderly through her hair. And wanting there to be no doubt about the depth of his feelings for her, he said, "So you could achieve your dream of resurrecting the business your father started and owning your own tearoom."

"And staying in Fort Worth to have my baby," Emily said happily. She gazed into his eyes.

Dan flashed a crooked smile. "That's really what you want?"

"Yes. My obstetrician is great. I love the hospital. I love the city. And I especially love being here with you and your family, seeing them—and you—every day." Emily sighed with contentment.

"You sure?" Dan asked as he kissed the sensitive spot behind her ear. "I thought you wanted to go home again."

Emily wound her arms around his neck and kissed him in all the familiar, wonderful ways they had both missed so much. "Home is where the heart is, Dan," she whispered. "And my heart is right here, with you." She drew the words from the deepest recesses of her soul.

Epilogue

Four and a half months later…

Everything was happening at once. "Where's the suitcase?" Walt demanded.

Kayla shrugged and held up the stopwatch. "I don't know. I thought you had it!"

Keys in hand, Tommy raced toward them. Breathless, he pointed to the SUV idling at the curb. "It's in the car!"

Walt looked around, frantic. "Next question. Where is the mother-to-be?"

Kayla eased the door open and peeked into the sanctuary. "She and Dad are still trying to get through their vows. But I think maybe they're done…'cause Dad just kissed Emily and it looks like she's kissing him back—"

"Are they crazy?" Ava cried, wringing her hands. She had thrown down her maid-of-honor bouquet and exited the chapel the moment Emily's first contraction hit. "We've got to get to the hospital!"

"We have time," Dan and Emily said in unison as they strolled leisurely down the aisle of the church.

"Plenty of it!" Emily reassured with maternal ease.

Everyone started to calm down.

Then Emily groaned and tightly gripped Dan's arm. By the time the second contraction in two minutes had passed, she straightened again. Face flushed, she murmured, "Or maybe not."

Dan steadied her. "Are you okay? I could call an ambulance."

"Just call Dr. Markham," Emily said as her body tensed and her face began to flush again.

"I'm on it!" Tommy shouted.

Kayla ran ahead to the SUV and yanked open the front passenger door. "Hurry, everybody! Hurry!"

"I think they might be a little excited," Dan said.

Laughing, Emily demurred. "I think so, too."

Three and a half hours later, the euphoria was even greater as Walt and the kids, still wearing their wedding finery, gathered around Emily's hospital bed to see the newest addition to the Kingsland clan.

"What a beauty!" Walt said, beaming.

"Perfect," Ava said.

"I think she is realllly cute," Kayla agreed as the newborn curled her fist around her little finger.

"A born athlete," Tommy decreed.

His sisters looked at him as if he was crazy. "How can you tell?" Ava asked.

"I just know." Tommy shrugged.

Gratitude flowing through her, Emily took in the familial scene. She'd always hoped to have four children—and a tall, blond, smart and sexy husband to love. And now, miraculously, she did. "I imagine this little one will be like her older siblings, able to do whatever she sets her mind to." Emily grinned at the newly official clan of hers.

"And her mommy and daddy," Dan added.

Together, he and Emily had more than proved that with hard work and determination all their dreams could come true.

Emily's partnership with Tex was proving to be a hit. The retail store at One Trinity River Place had opened on Valentine's Day and was doing a huge business, as was the tearoom. Chef for Hire was still going strong, as well— with personal chefs Emily had hired and now supervised.

Ava had been accepted at Harvard—the college of her choice—where she intended to study premed. Tommy planned to spend the summer working his first part-time job and attending wrestling camp. Kayla had just celebrated her ninth birthday and was learning to cook.

Walt had officially retired from his private investigative work so he would be free to help out with the new baby, as well as the kids.

And Dan…well, business had never been better.

His home life had never been better, either.

"So what are you going to name her?" Ava asked finally.

Dan and Emily exchanged looks.

"Bet you anything they've been thinking outside the box again," Tommy drawled.

"Please tell me it's not Wheelbarrow or some other completely weird name." Walt peered at them in comical trepidation.

Emily chuckled. "Not quite."

"Is it…Peaches?" Kayla asked, referring to some of the joke-names they'd bantered about the past months.

"Or…Trinity Place?" Tommy teased.

"Cornucopia?" Ava got into the joking spirit. "'Cause you all did meet in November!"

"Maybe it's Thanksgiving!" Kayla giggled.

"Thanksgiving Cornucopia Kingsland?" Tommy guessed.

"Nope. Not a one of those," Dan said.

Emily shifted the baby to one arm and linked hands with Dan. "Shall we tell them?" she asked.

Dan looked down at the baby in Emily's arms. She was without a doubt the most beautiful infant he'd ever seen, and the spitting image of her lovely, dark-haired, blue-eyed mother. And every bit as much a member of their family. "I guess we should," he said, since the moniker they'd picked out was perfect, after all.

Emily looked at the family gathered around. "We've decided to name her Grace, after my mother. And Rei—which means gratitude."

"We'll probably call her Gracie, for short," Dan added.

"Gracie Rei Kingsland." Tommy tried the name out.

"I like it!" Ava said.

"Me, too!" Kayla enthused.

"A fine and fitting Texas name," Walt said with another fond look at the infant. "Speaking of which, I think Miss Gracie looks all tuckered out. So we'll head out and let you three rest."

Kisses and hugs abounded.

Then it was just the three of them. Dan, Emily and the baby. Contentment flooded through him. He wasn't sure how it happened, but he had gotten everything he had ever wanted. And he was pretty sure Emily had, too.

She patted the bed beside her. "I know it's not Thanksgiving, but…"

Dan wrapped his arm around her shoulder, brought her against the curve of his body and settled next to her and Gracie Rei. "But it sure feels that way." He pressed a kiss to the top of Emily's head.

"We have so much to be grateful for," Emily acknowledged in a husky voice.

Dan kissed her again. "So much to cherish."

"There's only one thing we're lacking."

"What's that?"

"A proper honeymoon."

"Actually," Dan drawled, "I think I know just the place."

He left the bed long enough to retrieve his wedding suit jacket and remove a small wrapped box from the inside pocket. "I didn't have a chance to give you this."

Emily sent him a questioning glance as she handed him the baby and he gave her the gift and then warned, "I know I promised you I wouldn't make any more deals with Tex, but in this case, I figured you wouldn't mind."

Emily went very still.

"It's a gift from my heart," Dan said soberly. "And just so you know…everyone—Tex, Walt, the kids, even Brenda—is on board. We all want you to have this and we all felt you should be surprised."

"And to think," Emily murmured, mystified, "all I got you was the promise of a spectacular honeymoon to be taken later."

"Well, now you know where we'll go. Come on. Open it," Dan said.

With trembling fingers, Emily did so. Inside was a stack of glossy photos. So familiar…and yet not. "This is…!"

"The farm in Fredericksburg, where you grew up. I made a deal with Tex. While leaving the orchards and working parts of the farm intact, I expanded the house enough to make room for our entire family, and bought the ten acres surrounding it, too. So you can go home whenever you want. We can all go. For the occasional weekends and vacations—it'll be our special family retreat. As well as a very romantic place for just the two of us."

The new master suite, Emily noted, rifling through the photos, was especially luxurious. "You really did this?" she croaked, remembering the first time they'd made love there. She envisioned many more days and nights to come. "It's done?"

Dan nodded. Seeing Gracie Rei was once again sound asleep, he tenderly settled her in her hospital crib. "One hundred percent."

Tears of bliss rolled down Emily's face as she looked through photos of room after room. The care and time and attention it had taken to do all this, the fact that Dan truly got what the place meant to her… "Oh, Dan, I don't know what to say…except this is the best gift ever—and I love you."

"I love you, too." Slowly, they came together. Dan kissed her tenderly. "So what do you say?" He held her and gazed into her eyes. "Want to start planning our honeymoon—and our next family retreat? Heck, while we're at it, maybe a swimming pool and a play area in the backyard, too?"

Emily kissed him again, knowing life had never been better. And this was just the beginning! "I certainly do. But first—" she snuggled close to her husband, turning her face up to his "—I want to thank you for making all our dreams come true."

* * * * *

DADDY BY CHRISTMAS
by Patricia Thayer

Pregnant and alone, Mia starts to put her trust in property developer
Jackson. But when her past turns up to claim her, will her secrets
tear them apart?

CHRISTMAS MAGIC ON THE MOUNTAIN
by Melissa McClone

Sean didn't care who Zoe, the beauty on the mountain, was, just that
she would pretend to be his date for the holidays! Will the truth matter
after he falls in love?

CHRISTMAS AT BRAVO RIDGE
by Christine Rimmer

Devoted parents to their daughter, and good friends, Corrine and Matt
had their relationship sorted. But then an incredible night of passion
changed everything.

All the magic you'll need this Christmas…

When **Daniel** is left with his brother's kids, only one person can help. But it'll take more than mistletoe before **Stella** helps him…

Patrick hadn't advertised for a housekeeper. But when **Hayley** appears, she's the gift he didn't even realise he needed.

Alfie and his little sister know a lot about the magic of Christmas – and they're about to teach the grown-ups a much-needed lesson!

Available 1st October 2010

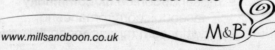

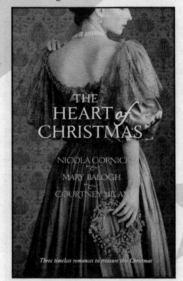
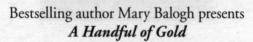

Bestselling author

PENNY JORDAN

presents

The Parenti Dynasty

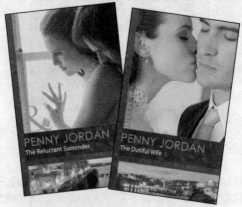

Power, privilege and passion
The worlds of big business and royalty unite…

The epic romance of Saul and Giselle begins with…

THE RELUCTANT SURRENDER
On sale October 2010

and concludes with

THE DUTIFUL WIFE
On sale November 2010

Don't miss it!

2 FREE BOOKS
AND A SURPRISE GIFT

We would like to take this opportunity to thank you for reading this Mills & Boon® book by offering you the chance to take TWO more specially selected books from the Cherish™ series absolutely FREE! We're also making this offer to introduce you to the benefits of the Mills & Boon® Book Club™—

- **FREE home delivery**
- **FREE gifts and competitions**
- **FREE monthly Newsletter**
- **Exclusive Mills & Boon Book Club offers**
- **Books available before they're in the shops**

Accepting these FREE books and gift places you under no obligation to buy, you may cancel at any time, even after receiving your free books. Simply complete your details below and return the entire page to the address below. You don't even need a stamp!

YES Please send me 2 free Cherish books and a surprise gift. I understand that unless you hear from me, I will receive 5 superb new stories every month, including two 2-in-1 books priced at £5.30 each, and a single book priced at £3.30, postage and packing free. I am under no obligation to purchase any books and may cancel my subscription at any time. The free books and gift will be mine to keep in any case.

Ms/Mrs/Miss/Mr _____ Initials _____

Surname _____

Address _____

_____

_____ Postcode _____

E-mail _____

Send this whole page to: Mills & Boon Book Club, Free Book Offer, FREEPOST NAT 10298, Richmond, TW9 1BR